First Printing Lock 'n Load Publishing Paperback Edition 2019
Copyright © 2019 Lock 'n Load Publishing, LLC.
All Rights Reserved.
Printed in the United States of America in the State of Colorado
Lock 'n Load Publishing LLC
1027 North Market Plaza, Suite 107 - 146
Pueblo West, Colorado, 81007
Rev 12
ISBN: 9-781733-104135

This novel is a work of fiction. All of the characters and events portrayed in this novel are either products of the authors' imagination or are used fictitiously.

CONTENTS

INTRODUCTION

Antony and Cleopatra. Lewis and Clark. Lennon and McCartney. Han and Chewbacca.

There's a certain appeal to the recurring theme of duos in human folklore and history. The best of these stories showcase the dynamics between two people who complement each other's weaknesses and strengths. These differences are what allows them to work together to accomplish great things. At the same time, they are also the forces that threaten to rip them apart. This tension makes the duo's fate unpredictable and keeps things interesting. In this book, you'll find several such pairings. Some of them succeed while others fail. Some are illusions while others are all too real.

"Army of Two" directly follows the events of "First Strike" though newcomers to the series should be able to enjoy this book without having read the first one. This book is a re-write but also an expanded edition of my previous book titled "Enemy Lines." After changing some details so it better fit into Keith Tracton's "World at War '85" setting, I saw greater potential for this book and ending up re-writing nearly all of it. "Army of Two" is an original story that lifts its own weight.

As I write this introduction, the "World at War '85" game is at the printers and is nearly ready to be shipped. From my occasional chats with David Heath and Keith Tracton, I've a strong impression that they are being careful to make sure the product is of the highest standards. The same is true of this book!

David gave me the time and freedom to take the story in this direction while Keith offered a sober look at a second draft that was too ambitious for its own good. Four more drafts led to the story you have in your hands right now and I'm quite proud of the result. I'm equally proud that these books serve as a companion to such a high-quality product as the boardgame.

Before I go, I need to thank several people who worked behind the scenes to make this book possible. A huge thanks goes out to Hans Korting, who has edited my books and offered constructive feedback. My sincere gratitude goes to Blackwell Hird, who always does a terrific job with layout.

Thanks to David Heath for the support throughout this project. A big thanks to Othello Lofton for lending your golden voice to the audiobook narration. Marc von Martial did an excellent job with the illustrations for this book and for that I am extremely grateful.

Last but not least, I offer my thanks to my family. My wife, Maya has been beyond patient and supportive throughout the writing of this book. My son, Hiroto, still hugs me even though dad hasn't been around much to play lately. Thank you, buddy!

Brad Smith
September 2019

PROLOGUE

Heaps of wounded men clung to the hull decks of the American armored personnel carriers that raced southwest in full retreat.

Two Soviet tanks a half kilometer away fired a pair of parting shots at the ragged column. Both rounds missed their targets, crashing instead into the opposite bank of the nearby river. The impacts sent fiery plumes of smoke and giant clumps of earth leaping up toward the iron gray sky.

Colonel Ted Mackinsky cursed as he watched the remnants of his task force scramble toward the only remaining bridge that led back west to the relative safety of friendly lines. Of the three companies under his command at the start of the battle, only Bravo was left. In all, he had a few battered M113s and a TOW Jeep.

Mackinsky barked out orders into the jeep's radio. No matter how much he yelled and swore, the ungainly procession of beaten troops refused to fix their jagged formation. He could hardly blame them. Bravo had gone through Hell and back in the last twenty minutes. Even the colonel, a combat veteran of a former war, had to suppress the urge to flee from this place of fire, death, and misery.

Mackinsky set the radio handset back in disgust and closed his eyes as the driver weaved the jeep through the knots of men and vehicles rushing for the safety of the nearby bridge.

As the engine roared and more rounds whooshed over the column, he soaked in the bad luck and poor decisions that had brought about such a monumental failure. How could everything have gone so poorly?

The mission had been simple– he was ordered to take three companies and conduct a counterattack against the Soviet flank to the north of Fulda City. The American force was to reclaim two captured bridges near the towns of Hemmen and Lüdermünd. Once that was done, the commander of the 8th Infantry Division was to pour reinforcements in to consolidate their hold on the objectives.

They never arrived. Soon after recovering from the initial blows, the Russians sent what must have been an entire armored battalion his way. Chaos ensued as the American victory was transformed into a messy defeat.

The Soviet counterattack was swift and unrelenting. Mackinsky lost all contact with two of his companies operating to the east of Lüdermünd.   Presumably, they had been overrun and were now dead.

When the T-80s charged at his position in the town, things were so messed up that Mackinsky was using the wrong call sign over the radio. Confusion added to the panic like jet fuel to a bonfire.

In a last-ditch effort to salvage things, Mackinsky told his fire support officer to call out "Broken Arrow" over the airwaves. In response, a hailstorm of American artillery slammed down on the outskirts of Lüdermünd at dangerous close range.

Though the oncoming Soviets suffered terribly, the fire mission had savaged the Americans. His only remaining Abrams was knocked out and not one of his soldiers was left uninjured by the blasts. The dust settled, and what little was left of the enemy force picked off the few American vehicles and infantry that remained. Now they were running for their lives.

Mackinsky took some satisfaction in knowing that a NATO airstrike would soon arrive to cover his retreat. Though the battle was already lost, he relished the thought of spiting the Russians with a rain of bombs from the sky. He recalled the words of Herman Melville as his jeep neared the bridge.

— X —

From Hell's heart, I stab at thee.

Halfway across the bridge, his jeep's radio crackled to life. A string of panicky words spat out over the static-filled airwaves:

FIREFOX MAIN TO WILDMAN … WITHDRAWING. OBJECTIVE KNIGHT… ENEMY TANKS IN SIGHT.

Mackinsky yelped and punched a fist in the air. Fox Troop was still out there! The radio message seemed to suggest that the cavalry unit was pulling back west toward Lüdermünd. The enemy tanks they had sighted were no doubt part of the Russian pursuit force that was headed his way right now.

If Fox could manage to fight its way through the gauntlet, they might join in the retreat. Though the battle was lost, there was still a chance to save American lives. Mackinsky's cautious optimism soon turned to dread.

The air strikes would be here any minute. Fox Troop would be caught out in the open when they hit. He broke out in a cold sweat at the horrifying prospect of his men and tanks incinerated by NATO planes.

Mackinsky roared over the handset.

THIS IS WILDMAN! DISENGAGE! AIR STRIKES INBOUND. DISENGAGE IMMEDIATELY!

No answer. He ordered the jeep to halt and gazed back east.

More than a dozen T-80s appeared along the top of the long ridge about half a kilometer away. Just behind the enemy tanks were scores of infantry running alongside. As they rushed down the slope toward Lüdermünd, Mackinsky's driver screamed.

"Sir! Blow the bridge now! Blow it or we're goners!"

Mackinsky knew the corporal was right. If the bridge remained standing, the pursuit force would chase them straight across the river and corner them. On the other hand, blowing it would trap Fox Troop on the east side of the river.

FIREFOX TO WILDMAN. ENGAGING ENEMY FORCES.

Fox Troop's M1 tanks drove along the ridgeline and fired deadly accurate shots down into the rear of the Soviet tank company. A T-80 erupted just as it reached the flat stretch of ground that lay between the hills and Lüdermünd. A fireball leapt from its turret ring and the vehicle shuddered to a halt.

A BMP was struck next. The whole thing flipped on its side and tumbled into a deep shell hole. Enemy ground troops were cut down by the Abrams' coaxial machineguns. The neat ranks of Russian soldiers collapsed like rows of wheat struck down by a scythe.

Despite such losses, the Soviets did not stop or slow down. Not one bit.

The last vehicles of Bravo Company reached the west side of the Fulda River. Mackinsky sat in the jeep and pondered the fate of Fox Troop. If he didn't call off the planes right now, they were doomed. Mackinsky turned to his driver and screamed.

"Get out!"

The corporal gawked at him as if the colonel had just grown a second head. Mackinsky repeated the order while shoving the man out of the vehicle and climbing over into the driver's seat. The only way to stop the airstrikes was to use the powerful long-range radio in the FIST vehicle.

Although there were plenty of short-range radios among the tanks and APCs of his task force, only the FIST had the ability to communicate with the airborne command aircraft that circled far overhead. Unfortunately, the FIST was back in Lüdermünd. The vehicle had been abandoned after it was damaged by the explosion of a nearby artillery round. He had to get to it. It was the only way.

Without bothering to explain, he threw the jeep into gear and drove straight back east across the bridge. As he crossed to the other side, he lifted the radio handset and tuned the frequency to speak with Captain Harris, the commander of Bravo.

THIS IS WILDMAN. BLOW THE BRIDGE! CODEWORD CHECKMATE!

The force of the ensuing blast was enough to levitate the jeep for a split second. The ground welled up underneath and heaved like a ship in rough seas. Behind him, the bridge crumbled. Huge concrete chunks tumbled into the rushing waters of the Fulda. Mackinsky was trapped on the east side of the river. His fate was now tied with that of Fox Troop.

The jeep swerved and leaned up on two wheels as he swung the steering wheel hard to the left. Mackinsky's vehicle bounded over the uneven ground just outside of Lüdermünd.

Fifty yards inside the town limits, he spotted the stricken FIST lying on its side on a mound of rubble. The jeep squealed to a halt and he dismounted.

A machinegun popped off a steady drumbeat of rounds in the distance. Little fountains of dust kicked up near his feet as he ran. Spasms of terror clutched at his muscles. Mackinsky battled the instinct to dive to the ground.

He grunted and strained the final yards to his destination. Though it seemed he should already be at the FIST, his legs pumped in slow motion as though he were in a nightmare. Wading through the thick heavy air, he gulped down ragged breaths then wrenched opened the FIST vehicle's rear ramp and dove inside.

On hands and knees, he groped along the hard metal floor of the dark interior. When at last he sensed the radio headset in his grasp, a surge of relief nourished the tiny but growing sense that he just might succeed in calling off the airstrike. Two fingers stabbed at the radio transceiver's power button and Mackinsky heard himself cackle as its cracked crimson light blinked on.

Two turns of the dial were enough to tune the set to the right frequency. The words leapt out of him too fast at first. He stumbled over the consonants like a drunk at closing time. After briefly admonishing himself, Mackinsky gathered his wits together and spoke again – this time with grammar-school enunciation.

ALL AIR UNITS! THIS IS BEARCLAW. ABORT. I SAY AGAIN – ABORT YOUR MISSION! FRIENDLIES ARE IN THE TARGET AREA.

A hiss of static was the only response. Mackinsky scanned the floor around him and picked up a trail of loose and broken wires that connected the handset to the radio. The damn thing was broke. No wonder they hadn't heard him!

His sweat-slick fingers worked feverishly to tie the loose ends back together. It was hard to see in the dim light of the vehicle, so he took his best guess as to which wire went where. After twenty seconds of practicing blind supposition and baseless optimism, his makeshift repair job was deemed "good enough."

Ted Mackinsky got on the radio again and demanded the impending airstrike be aborted.

Without intending it, he found himself cursing over the airwaves and promising grievous bodily harm to any pilot who so much as thought about dropping their ordnance near here.

Mackinsky set the radio down and gathered the courage to return outside to find better cover. As he stood, an ear-shattering metallic clang signified the loss of his jeep. A jet engine whined and a giant hammer blow struck down upon the earth.

The gale-force impact ripped apart Mackinsky's senses. In the next instant, he was flung headlong against the interior wall. The steel hull rushed toward him like a speeding locomotive.

Everything went black.

AN ARMY OF TWO

BRAD SMITH

LIFE DURING WARTIME

7 km North of Fulda

Sergeant Will Harland lay on the grass and watched the world burn. Acrid smoke drew into his lungs with each labored breath. Thick wet coughs welled up within his chest and squeezed out of his throat. Just fifty meters away sat his M1 Abrams tank. Surrounding it were the mangled bodies of men who were dead or dying.

The wall of flames drew closer. With it came a searing heat that pressed in on him like a vice.

Harland's brain commanded his arms and legs to move, but the orders went unheeded. The realization that he felt nothing below his waist smothered the embers of thought that floated through his mind.

The idea of burning to death here alone on this ravaged hillside threatened to overthrow the fragile internal order of his mind and body. In an effort to quell the mounting insurrection of panic, he tried to remember. Fragments of the recent past assembled in his mind.

First, came the pungency of cordite and the way it stung his nose as he fired the Abrams' main gun. It was accompanied, as always, by the tremble of his seat and the chatter of teeth.

For a moment, there was a fracturing of sensation – a feeling of floating up and out of his own body. A high-pitched note pierced his ears then faded as the world reassembled itself in familiar patterns of light and dark, sound and silence.

Next came the whoops and hollers of his fellow crewmembers. The BMP in his sights was eviscerated. Giant chunks of the vehicle lay scattered all around its carcass. Along with the other men in the Abrams, Harland was awash in a supreme kind of relief mixed with something akin to joy – not at the enemy's death, but at the fact that they were still alive. The tank and the men were rhythmically aligned. Victory seemed all but assured.

Then there were the frantic shouts as the tank threw a track. The rest of the crew dismounted and then -.

Nothing.

Harland's thoughts veered into the same mental lanes as most dying men. His mother's smile. A first kiss. The elusive face of a childhood friend.

As he waited for the flames to consume him, a pair of burly arms wrapped around his torso and dragged him away from the conflagration. Harland hadn't even the energy to utter a thanks. Instead, he closed his eyes and let exhaustion overtake him. The hollow emptiness of slumber offered a reprieve from his pain-wracked body.

When Harland awoke, the sun's harsh rays stabbed at his half-lidded eyes. As his sight slowly returned, he found himself alone in a field littered with corpses and charred vehicles. The rage of last night's inferno was gone, replaced by the melancholy stillness of sunrise over a shell-battered landscape. Everything around him was blanketed by the bitter gray tones of ash.

Somewhere off in the distance came the snarl of a diesel engine. And though he wasn't sure exactly why, this unnatural sound registered as a threat.

"Get up," he croaked. His voice was raspy and coated in uneven tones of ache and fatigue. "Get up or you're dead."

With a deep groan, he rolled over onto his stomach and whimpered before pushing up with both hands. As he did so, a stabbing pain shot through his right arm.

For the first time, he noticed a blood-drenched bandage wrapped neatly around the bicep. Who had done that? The answer would have to wait. Someone was coming and it was time to get away from here.

Harland managed to throw his body upright by using his good arm. Like a toddler taking his first steps, the 25-year-old man wobbled and then collapsed to the hard earth. After several long minutes and countless failed attempts, he finally stood on two shaky but firm legs.

The first tentative steps around the still battlefield pulled his thoughts to the stacks of corpses that lay everywhere. It was nearly impossible to tell which side they had been on. Some men were burnt beyond recognition. Others were covered in the mud and blood of battle.

Harland pilfered a half-filled canteen from one of the bodies and lifted it to his cracked lips. The cool water slid down his sandpaper throat and a serenity settled over him. The mutter of engines he heard minutes ago was now gone. For that, Harland was relieved and more than a little perplexed.

He leaned against the blackened hull of a T-80 and let the ragged morning sing its vile harmonies. Dying men groaned. Artillery guns boomed. Combat aircraft criss-crossed the skies far above. All at once, the question came to him like an unstoppable flood that drowned his self-pity and deadened the sting of his wounded arm.

What the hell happened here?

He recalled that NATO was at war with the Soviets. The Russians invaded West Germany. Things had gone badly for the Americans and they had fallen back again and again from the border.

Like a jigsaw puzzle hurled against a wall, scattered fragments of yesterday lay strewn around in the punch-drunk haze of his brittle mind. He knew his name, rank, and unit – all of these were helpfully sewn on his fatigues. He was Sergeant William P. Harland from the 8th Infantry Division.

That was a good start.

He rummaged through his belongings to check for any other clues. Tucked away in his left breast pocket was a tattered copy of a Stephen King novel called "The Dead Zone."

He knew it well. Harland had always loved stories and this was one of his favorites.

It was about a guy who could touch someone and glimpse their past or future. Just like that, all their darkest secrets were revealed. Harland wished he had such a power right now - at least he might stand a chance of figuring out what the hell he was doing here.

Inside the book's cover were notes scrawled in his own chicken-scratch:

Operation First Strike

Task Force Lance

Counterattack – Fulda. Lüdermünd.

8ID*D/2*68/2 (Delta) – Queen

2/11 ACR (Fox) - King

8ID*B/3*8/1 (Bravo) – Rook

He tried to work out the jumble of letters and numbers but nothing made sense. It was like trying to piece together an entire bag of shredded cheese.

When he flipped to the back of the book and found his crudely drawn map of the operation, everything dropped into place. Harland let a lazy smile crawl across his face.

He was part of a counterattack aimed at the Soviet flank to the north of Fulda. The objective of Task Force Lance, commanded by Colonel Theodore Mackinsky, had been to take back the bridges around Lüdermünd.

To that end, the 8th Infantry Division had contributed two companies – Delta (Harland's company) and Bravo – to work together with Fox Troop from 2/11 Armored Cavalry Regiment. The objectives were named after chess pieces. The town of Lüdermünd was "Rook" while two large hills to the east of it had been dubbed "King" and "Queen".

Things went well enough in the beginning of the mission, but the unexpected presence of civilians in Lüdermünd had delayed the operation. Harland's own company – Delta – was slammed by a wave of T-80 tanks near Objective Queen as they waited for Bravo's Captain Harris to mop up the Russians at Objective Rook.

As for Harland's tank, most of the crew of The Terminator had been dismounted when the Russians hit back.

While the three other men had gone to check on the tank's broken rear drive sprocket, two platoons of T-80s ambled over the nearest hill and opened fire.

Harland remembered the bodies of his fellow crewmembers thrown into the air by the blast of a tank round. As the only man inside the Abrams, he did what he was trained to do. He fired back. One of the enemy tanks blew up and then a whole bunch of them shot at him from point-blank range.

The playback of memories screeched to a halt. Harland scooped an AKM and two magazines up off the ground. He had never fired a Soviet weapon before but this one seemed almost intuitive in its simplicity. A burlap bag with two grenades clattering around in the bottom was enough to complete his kit.

With a rough idea of where he was and what had happened, Harland faced west and resolved to find friendly territory. Harland wasn't sure how he would get there, but he knew that staying around here was probably dangerous. He aimed his aching body in a westerly direction and limped toward home.

WHO IS IT

Harland stood near the crest of the hill with his jaw hung wide open. On the way up here, he wasn't sure what he would find – maybe he'd glimpse a bunch of American tanks and trucks filled with guys who would be glad to see him. Or maybe he'd spot a bunch of Soviets that he would need to run away from.

Instead, he was greeted by the sight of utter destruction - Biblical in its proportions.

From here to the riverbank, every mark of civilization had been torn asunder. The gnarled wreckage of tanks and vehicles was strewn among yawning craters. Thick curls of oily smoke snaked upwards, blotting out the sun and casting a malevolent pall upon the gloomy scene.

Harland had wondered earlier about who had won yesterday's battle. Now the answer was plain to see – nobody.

When he saw that the bridges to the north and southwest of the town had been blown, his gut twisted in despair. There was no choice left but to swim across. The idea of trudging through the West German countryside soaking wet and without a map hardly appealed to him. But what choice did he have?

A twig snapped.

Harland swiveled and froze at the sight of a tall man in tattered US Army fatigues and a case of five o'clock shadow to match. His hands were clamped around an M16 rifle.

The barrel was pointing straight at Harland's chest.

"Move and you're dead."

Harland's eyes wandered to the chevrons on the man's collar. A master sergeant. Harland thanked the heavens above. The last thing he needed was to be wandering behind enemy lines with an officer in tow.

"Hey. I'm on your side," he said. "Name's Harland. Sergeant."

The rifle lowered and the grizzled man growled back at him. "Franklin."

Harland stepped in to shake hands. Franklin made no move to reciprocate. He just stared at Harland like he was crazy.

"You were with Fox Troop?" asked Harland.

"I-I'm not even sure how I got here.."

"Someone saved me last night," said Harland. "The flames…I was a goner." He pointed to the bandage on his arm. "Was it you who patched me up?"

"You're dreamin'," said Franklin. After a pause, the master sergeant jerked a thumb to the west.

"Time to get moving, soldier."

"What's the plan?" asked Harland. "You think we can get over to the other side of that river and find some friendlies?"

Franklin nodded to the south. For the first time, Harland caught a glimpse of the long snaking lines of military vehicles that sat backed up behind Fulda.

"The Soviets are rerouting their military traffic to the south near Fulda for now," said the master sergeant. "My guess is they'll have some engineers here soon enough to clean up and rebuild their defenses. If we can beat them to the punch and get across that river in time, we might have a chance to make it west. I take it you can swim?"

"I'm not Aquaman," said Harland. "But I can doggy paddle with the best of them."

Both men trudged down the long slope toward the hellscape that lay waiting. Every step of the way, Harland wondered if Franklin was his savior or a liability. It occurred to him that Franklin was no doubt asking himself the same question.

When Harland arrived at the base of the hill, the stench from the nearby town was enough to make him gag. Even though he had grown up around pig farms all his life, it was hard to stomach this bitter wind and the horror it presaged.

Harland cast his eyes upon the stretch of ground that lay between the base of the hill and the town of Lüdermünd to the west. The intervening landscape was characterized by gaping craters and shattered trees – an apocalyptic sight that resembled a darkened wasteland from some Tolkien novel.

Harland shuddered as he scanned the horizon, made surreal and foreign by the scale and extent of its ugliness. Am I alive or dead? Is this Hell?

To the northwest lay the town of Hemmen. There were fewer wrecks along the way and the ground was more even.

Harland pointed in the direction of the town.

"How about that way?"

Franklin shot back a response.

"Negative."

Harland didn't ask why. Franklin just seemed to know what he was doing. They started off toward Lüdermünd.

Not twenty paces later, a tracer zipped over their heads. Harland hit the dirt as Franklin shouted and charged forward. Harland lifted his AKM and squeezed off short shaky bursts of return fire.

When the magazine was dry, Harland crawled a dozen yards toward the lip of a nearby crater. A charred T-80 tank sat along its downward slope. The ruined turret was perched at an angle like a jaunty sailor's cap. He took giant gulping breaths as his arms and legs scraped against the hard patch of ground underneath.

Harland reached the cover of the tank and leaned over, hoping to catch a glimpse of his attackers. A dozen rounds smacked against the steel hull. Harland flinched. All doubts about the seriousness of his predicament vanished. Harland was pinned down. He was also alone.

When the shooting dissipated, he popped up and pointed his weapon in the direction of the enemy fire. Harland squeezed the trigger of the AKM only to be rewarded with a click. As if in response, an orange tracer whooshed inches from his head like a tiny comet.

Harland fumbled with the rifle in a vain effort to clear the jam. No dice. The weapon was filthy and the breech was clogged with dirt. He would need to fieldstrip and clean the piece of junk. No time for that. He tossed the weapon aside in disgust.

"Hey!" Franklin screamed at him from twenty yards to his right.

Harland ventured a peek over the lip of his crater to see his ally prone behind a low berm. Franklin fired off a short burst in the direction of a wrecked BMP then gestured toward Harland's burlap bag. A series of hand signals followed as gunfire crackled.

"Go!" screamed Franklin. "Go now!"

Harland clutched the bag and scrambled forward to get within throwing distance of the enemy. Enemy rounds bit into the ground all around him. Occasionally, one of them would dig into the dirt and send a spray of pebbles at his face.

Every yard he gained was like a small miracle. Someone watching might have called him courageous, but Harland just felt stupid. During the entire ordeal, he cursed and swore while his anger grew at Franklin for sending him on this suicidal journey.

When he at last reached a clump of rocks, Harland curled up in a ball and shook as the rivers of adrenaline coursed through his body. Somewhere behind him, Franklin drilled out an entire magazine of rounds with his M16 set to fully automatic.

"I'm dry!" he shouted.

Harland's heart fell as he reached into the burlap bag and dug out both grenades. Three failed attempts at trying out for the varsity baseball team flashed through his mind as he studied the shattered BMP. Was he good enough to lob a grenade behind it? Coach Stinson would have despaired.

Harland pulled the pin and sent the little green ball sailing through the air. It flew in a graceful arc, only to slap against the hull of the BMP and bounce off. The grenade exploded harmlessly ten yards from where he had intended it to land.

A pair of shots zinged against Harland's stony cover. He teetered on the brink of all-out panic and would have given in but for the fact he had one grenade left. As he held it, he made a promise to himself. If this misses, it's time to wave the white flag.

Harland tossed the grenade. It disappeared behind the vehicle, right where he had intended it to land. From somewhere in the back of his mind came the rapturous applause of a hundred little league dads. A sharp stabbing agony radiated along his bicep.

Three seconds were followed by a mocking stillness. Gradually, the awful truth unfolded in Will Harland's head. He had thrown the grenade beautifully – and it had turned out to be a dud.

Well, he had tried.

Harland gathered what little strength remained and racked his brains to find the Russian words for surrender. Nothing came. They were way back in the little phrase book he kept in The Terminator's scorched right bustle, along with all the rest of his kit.

Before he could croak out the words in English, he heard a sharp crack. A torrent of fragments was thrown upwards by the blast of his grenade.

Franklin ran forward and rounded the side of the vehicle. After a few seconds, he waved over at Harland, who went to look for himself at what had happened. In the dirt, lay a pair of dead Russians.

"Guess it was a Friday afternoon at the grenade factory," said Franklin.

Harland stared at the bodies. They weren't the first Russians he had killed in this war, but it was the first time he had come this close to seeing the effects of what he had done.

He had half-expected to feel a sense of shame or guilt. Instead, there was just a sort of blank numbness that swam through his mind. He had survived the ordeal and they hadn't. There was a brutal simplicity to it.

Franklin collected the rifles from the dead.

"There's no way Ivan didn't hear that gunfight," he said. "We need to get moving before they send more guys."

A two-minute jog brought both men near the remains of Lüder-münd. Blasted T-80s intermingled with the metal carcasses of M1 Abrams tanks. It was plain from both the scale of destruction and the close proximity of dead enemy and friendly units that someone had called artillery down on their own heads.

When they clambered up the first mound of high rubble, the culprit became clear enough – a FIST artillery observer vehicle sat there toppled on its side. The tin can was dented and the tracks were completely ripped off. It looked as though someone had tossed it around like a child's toy.

"Might be a radio inside," said Franklin. "We can call for a pick-up." He stepped over to the FIST and examined the rear ramp.

From somewhere to the east, vehicle engines rumbled. It sounded as though they were climbing the nearby hills, straining to get over the long slopes.

"Time to go," said Harland.

"Help me out with this! It's stuck."

"We need to get out of here," said Harland. "Someone's coming this way."

Franklin jammed the butt of his rifle into the gap between the ramp and the hull. The ramp squealed open and the master ser-geant disappeared inside.

Harland's heart fell as he watched a huge Ural truck bumble over the crest of the hill to the east. Though its progress was slowed by driving around the numerous craters and wrecks, it would be here very soon.

"Franklin, those are Russians! We need to go now."

"Hey, I think this guy's alive! Help me out here."

Harland stared at the gentle flowing waters of the Fulda River only a hundred meters away.

There was still time to make it there and maybe even get across before the Russians arrived. As he limped, the bandage on his arm itched and he remembered that someone had bothered to stop and save him last night from the choking smoke and searing flames.

And now he was about to repay it by abandoning somebody. To Hell with that.

He turned back. Twenty paces took him inside the darkened and cramped interior of the FIST where a body lay.

"Radio's broken. But this guy here is still breathing," said Franklin. "I heard him groan."

"Hey," said Harland. "There are enemy vehicles coming here and we are gonna get lit if we stay here."

Franklin shrugged.

"We can't just leave this guy. Help me move him."

Harland wrapped his good arm around the soldier's stocky legs and mentally shelved the concerns about how they were going to cross the river with a wounded man.

As each second passed, the window of opportunity for escape was rapidly closing. He cursed his conscience. If Harland had just gone for the river when he had the chance, he would be as good as home by now.

Franklin gestured to set the wounded man down. Harland studied the weathered and filthy face. His eyes were red and swollen and a trail of dried blood emerged from a long gash that snaked along his forehead.

There was something familiar about the graying mustache and buzz cut. A glance at the bird on his collar confirmed his suspicions. The man in front of him was none other than Colonel Ted Mackinsky – the leader of Task Force Lance.

Will Harland had trudged half a mile through hell and nearly died in a hail of gunfire only to find the highest ranking American officer this side of the Fulda River.

It didn't take a genius to figure out what the Russians would do if they found him here alive. They would torture every ounce of information out of him before either executing him or sending him to some godforsaken prison camp.

Harland watched another pair of Urals crest the hill to the east and descend the slope. They were coming straight for Lüdermünd. He turned to Franklin.

"What do we do?"

The master sergeant slapped a fresh magazine in his pilfered rifle.

"I'll hold them off here. You go see if you can get some help."

"Are you sure?" asked Harland. "You're way outnumbered."

Franklin glowered.

"I'm not sure at all, Will. So you better go before I change my mind. You come back here again and I'll shoot you myself."

With a heavy heart, Harland staggered toward the river. The trucks squealed to a halt behind him and gunshots rang out. Moments later, he stood on the muddy bank of the Fulda River. Could he really swim across?

Harland took a long breath and leapt into the dusky waters.

TAKE ME TO THE RIVER

Harland was drowning. His limbs had grown numb and the powerful current swept him further downstream as he flailed. Every foot of progress toward the safety of the opposite bank was purchased with a mile's worth of exertion.

Sapped of energy, he was dragged below the surface. Long drafts of water gushed down his throat and cut off his breath. Some part of him found the wherewithal to do the only thing that would help him survive a minute longer. He laid back in an attempt to claim buoyancy. Coughing and spluttering, his body broached the surface.

By making furtive motions with his arms and legs, he angled his body in the direction of the current. Afraid of slamming into a rock, Harland raised his head to catch a glimpse of whatever lay ahead. A branch jutted out from the nearby riverbank.

Harland reached up with his arms like field goal posts. His palms smacked painfully into the wood while needle-like thorns pricked his fingers. The current yanked at his body in an effort to reclaim him. Though he was mostly spent, Harland refused to give in.

He tightened his grip around the branch and inched along its length toward the nearby bank. Hand over hand, he made gradual progress. Somewhere in the back of his mind, Drill Instructor Rasmussen screamed at him.

"Get moving, scumbag! You want to quit and go home to mommy?! Be my guest!"

Halfway to safety, the base of the branch shook loose from the muddy soil that anchored it to the river's edge. The limb cracked then split under his weight. Harland plummeted. The river took him once again.

He did not have the energy for despair. Resigned to his fate, he let nature claim its bounty. The cold rushing water sucked him under. Harland offered not the slightest note of resistance to its whims.

The embrace of eternal slumber never came. Instead, Harland was yanked bodily from the river like a fish caught in a net and dragged him to shore. Though he had finally reached his goal, Harland took no comfort.

On the contrary, Harland's world rang with the hollering of outraged men – remorseless figures who possessed not a trifle of sympathy for his rotten predicament.

He had dealt with these kinds of people before. They lurked in the dark corners of every life. Theirs was a world that was neatly divided into weak and strong. The former was an affront to nature. Only the latter had won the right to exist. Their currency was misery - and to Harland, they would dole it out in abundance.

A boot stamped down hard in the small of his back. Next came a punch to the head joined by a series of thunderous blows along his spine. Someone turned him over onto his back.

Howling waves of agony tore through his groin as they kicked and jabbed at him. And when they finally paused, it was only to laugh at his humiliation before they continued the beating afresh. Mercy seemed a cruel joke – a concept that belonged to a forgotten time and a place.

A door slammed shut in Harland's mind.

PEOPLE LIKE US

Captain Peter Mackinsky watched the hilly terrain shoot past outside the Blackhawk's window. The ground writhed with fire and destruction and masses of vehicles snaking toward the frontlines.

He spared a thought for his father, a colonel with the 8th Infantry Division. The old man was somewhere down there, commanding men and tanks to take on the Soviets, who were pushing ever deeper into West Germany.

Like a thief in the night, war had erupted without warning. Only a month ago, Peter had spent two blissful weeks' worth of leave with his father, fishing and hunting near the Appomattox River. As avid outdoorsmen, life could not have been more peaceful or idyllic. Now billions of lives just like his were disrupted as the course of history spun off into wild and unpredictable directions.

Tanner nudged Mackinsky's shoulder and leaned in close to shout a question.

"What's the guy's name again?"

Mackinsky hollered back over the chatter of the rotors.

"Brandt. B-R-A-N-D-T," he said. "Major. East German Army,"

"And he's a good guy?"

Mackinsky chuckled at the naiveté of the question while he nodded. Good. Bad. Who thought like that anymore? Tanner had obviously watched Star Wars one too many times. Then again, maybe that made the fighting and dying easier.

A stream of baseball-sized anti-aircraft fire blew past the window. The helicopter banked hard right and Mackinsky shifted his weight to compensate. The whole machine rattled as it swung back left again. Mackinsky's stomach lurched and he fought the urge to retch up a cold breakfast.

Bates leaned over and puked. The young man's broad sweat-soaked face was bloated with near-panic. Mackinsky wasn't surprised. The guy was strung higher than a trapeze line. That was no crime, but it was obvious from the way he jumped at every noise and spoke in rapid-fire sentences that Bates wasn't coping well. Mackinsky chided himself for failing to notice it earlier. *I should have let him sit this one out.*

In truth, the whole team was on edge and still in the throes of fresh grief. The last mission had whittled them down from eight men to four. Collins and Miller had both been killed by a direct artillery hit. Davidson's brains were splattered by a sniper. Bradley was taken out by the Hind helicopter he was busy trying to shoot down. All of them were good men. None of them deserved to die.

Upon requesting replacements, the team's commanding officer, Colonel Evans, had been informed that losses were bad across the board. They would just have to make do. It was the same old runaround and it shocked no one. US V Corps had treated special operations like a disowned child since the war began.

Manny flicked open his eyes. Without saying anything, the big man smiled and said something that made Bates grin. Mackinsky looked away, afraid that staring might spoil the act of camaraderie.

When it was time, Mackinsky held up his headset for his fellow operators to see and plugged it into the wall port. The others took their cue and did the same.

"Let's go over the plan again," he said.

An alarm warbled somewhere in the cockpit and the Blackhawk trembled like a leaf in a summer storm. Mackinsky gulped down the terror and continued.

"Objective?"

Darren Tanner's thin bony hand shot up.

"Retrieve supply sked from Depot Seven."

"Correct," said Mackinsky. "And what's the significance of the sked?"

The Blackhawk soared up the steep slope of a hill and Mackinsky's hand wrapped around the edge of the bench to keep from being thrown forward. Tanner spoke again.

"The 'sked' is a schedule of resupply. It lets NATO commanders figure out which Pact units at the front are shortest on things like ammunition and fuel. That means they could plan counterattacks against the most vulnerable units with a greater chance of success."

"Bingo," said Mackinsky. "Where is the 'sked' for Supply Depot 7 likely located?"

Manny boomed into the microphone. "East Germany. Wolfsburg."

"Okay," said Mackinsky. "Care to narrow that down?"

Bates' voice shook as he answered. "Commander's office. South side of the compound."

Mackinsky recalled the briefing. Evans had hinted that a double agent had risked his life to pinpoint the sked's precise location. He took a second to wonder at the man's fate. Tanner had asked but the colonel simply lowered his eyes and changed the subject.

As if they were on a rollercoaster ride, the helicopter began a steep descent. Mackinsky was shoved backward in his seat. The rotor gave off a high-pitched warble and he was sure they were about to crash.

Moments later, the helicopter leveled out.

"How are we getting in there?" Mackinsky asked.

"We grab a vehicle stolen by a friendly East German insurgent group headed by Werner Braun," said Tanner.

"Correction. Our contact's name is Werner Brandt," said Mackinsky. "Werner von Braun is the rocket scientist. I think he's dead now."

Mackinsky remembered the dossier he'd been shown. The lean handsome figure in a military uniform was the esteemed leader of an insurgent group operating in the Bezirk-Magdeburg area.

Brandt was a cunning and ruthless infantry officer who had spent his entire adult life leading a double existence. While presenting himself as almost fanatically loyal to Soviet communism, the major had kept hidden his hatred of all things Russian.

The CIA took a chance and courted Brandt during the early years of his mandatory military service. A long talk convinced the major that the best way to hurt East Germany's Communist overlords was by working from the inside. Like many other secret dissidents, the man was put to use as a double agent and earmarked as the leader of a covert anti-communist insurgent group should World War III break out.

When the balloon went up, two Special Forces veterans were yanked back into service and would be here in a few days to advise Brandt. The whole idea was laughable to Mackinsky, who saw it as yet another cheap and poorly designed method of creating trouble in the enemy's backyard. Instead of dropping a ton of resources and manpower into East Germany, the CIA and DIA were content to bring in two fossils who hadn't seen action in nearly two decades.

Mackinsky's headset crackled to life and the co-pilot's silky-smooth voice piped up.

"Get ready," he said. "Drop zone in two."

The four operators in the passenger compartment made a final check of their gear and weapons. Mackinsky pulled his man-pack radio from the secure wall mount and sighed. A fist-sized hole had been punched clean through it. The radio was busted beyond repair.

Mackinsky's heart fell as he looked around. The Blackhawk's cabin had been punctured by so many bullets that it resembled a block of Swiss cheese. How many other things were broken? There was no time to check.

The Blackhawk tore around the last hill and skimmed the tree-tops before passing over a farmhouse and a barn. Just as it reached a clearing, the helicopter flared into a hover then dropped.

A meter above the waist-high grass, Mackinsky jumped out and took up a perimeter with the rest of his men. In a matter of seconds, the Blackhawk lifted a dozen meters and shot west out of sight.

Mackinsky scanned the tree line for any sign of Brandt or his insurgents. At the edge of the forest came a flash of movement. He let out a short sharp whistle and waited, unsure if he would be met by the counter-signal or a hail of gunfire.

A high-pitch trill punctured the air. Mackinsky peered through a pair of binoculars and spotted a figure wearing East German combat fatigues crouched amid the undergrowth. Hand signals were exchanged and when it was evident that it was safe, the four Americans jogged to the line of tall pine trees that dominated the low surrounding hills.

A middle-aged man with salt-and-pepper hair and a weathered face strode toward them. A rifle was slung over his shoulder.

"Brandt," he said.

Mackinsky shook the offered hand. "You know, you really should have more security out here to greet us," he said.

The major said nothing. His face turned red and the scowl deepened.

"You got the BMP?" asked Mackinsky.

"Yes. At great risk to my men's lives. We have it for you."

Mackinsky pointed to Brandt's distinctive fatigues. The loose-fitting jacket and pants were olive green and covered with short vertical lines. A forage cap was perched on his head, with a button-like patch of the East German hammer and compass sewn to its fore.

"And the uniforms?"

Brandt scooped up a brown paper bag from the ground and tossed it at Mackinsky, who opened it to find three sets of East German Army fatigues. Manny wouldn't need them – he would be out of sight and covering the rest of the team from afar.

Tanner, Bates, and Mackinsky suited up. Brandt and a few of his men adjusted the fatigues and combat webbing until their appearance adhered to an acceptable East German military standard.

Once they were presentable, Mackinsky and his men handed their belongings off to Brandt. The East German major ran a hand along one of the M16 rifles the Americans had brought along to exchange for East German weapons.

"It's like a toy!" said Brandt.

"It'll put a hole in your face just the same," said Bates.

"Keep them," said Mackinsky.

"Not nearly enough," growled Brandt. "My men and I are sharing weapons! Each of us has only fifty rounds of ammunition.

How am I supposed to start a revolution?"

Mackinsky threw up his hands. "I'm aware of your issues, major. Not my zoo. Not my monkeys. I'm sure you'll get all that good stuff when your advisers arrive."

Brandt paced back and forth like a tiger in a cage.

"And what if we get attacked in the meantime? I cannot set up a proper defense around our encampment. It's impossible to send out patrols!"

"I'll talk to my boss when we get back," said Mackinsky. "Sorry, major. Best I can do."

Brandt trudged off into the thick forest. The East German insurgents followed all around them, shooting glares in the Americans' direction. Mackinsky felt naked. Here they were in enemy territory, surrounded by angry armed men.

To Mackinsky's complete lack of surprise, the agency had made promises that were not being kept. It would be so easy for Brandt to kidnap the team and make demands of their benefactors. Or better yet, they could just turn the Americans over to the East German government in exchange for a promise of amnesty and perhaps even a reward.

If Brandt was having second thoughts about this whole situation, he had just been handed a clear way out. Mackinsky looked back at his fellow team members and raised an eyebrow. Manny and the others gave quick nods in return. Though the American team leader hadn't uttered a word, the message was loud and clear.

Be ready.

Mackinsky and his men stayed laser-focused on the East Germans as they continued their tense journey through the bush. When they finally arrived at a clearing with a BMP sitting in the middle of it, Mackinsky waved off his concerns about a potential betrayal by Brandt. The man had delivered.

The squat fighting vehicle looked as if it had been through Hell and back. The skirt on the left side dangled from the hull as though it had given up. Dark scorch marks lined the deck and the turret had several dents, as if someone had pounded on it with a giant sledgehammer.

The paint job was a mere suggestion of its original color. Brown rust bit into the edges of the frame, lending it all the visual appeal of a decaying tooth.

"We needed a BMP," said Bates. "Not a garbage can."

Mackinsky squeezed his eyes shut and braced himself for Brandt's fury, but Tanner's high-pitched laugh defused the tension. The East German major's scowl softened and out came a hearty chuckle.

Manny walked over and ran a hand over the steel shell of the vehicle then pulled on the handle of the rear hatch. As it squealed open, a stench resembling rotten dog food spilled through the air of the clearing.

Mackinsky peered inside with a flashlight while holding his nose. The seats were torn and errant wires hung from the roof here and there. The interior walls of the vehicle were corroded and brown.

"Was this thing…on fire at some point?" Bates asked.

Brandt shrugged.

"TWENTY TWO liberated it from the junkyard near a motor pool. It was no small effort to retrieve it."

Mackinsky remembered the briefing. The men in these groups were anonymous. Instead of names, they used numbers to refer to one another. That way, their identities – and families - were protected, even if someone in the group turned traitor or was captured. The only man who kept his identity was Brandt, who had no living relatives.

The engine coughed to life, much to the delight of the Americans. Mackinsky considered the risk that Brandt and his men had taken in order to secure the vehicle. That they had managed to do so with a few weapons and a handful of ammunition was more than dangerous – it was asking way too much.

"You know, Brandt," he said. "We're hitting a supply dump. I'll grab what I can for you. No promises, though."

The major shot a look over his way and the corners of his lips budged upward.

"I should like that very much," he said.

Bates shook his head and Mackinsky knew instantly what was being communicated. The attempt would incur extra risks for the team. Already, they were pushing too hard. Mackinsky knew it was crazy to take on more danger, but this just felt right. He wanted to help.

Mackinsky pulled out a tattered map and pointed at a location halfway between the supply depot and the pickup zone.

"If we get something, we'll dump it off here for you. Got it?"

The four Americans piled into the BMP. Mackinsky stood in the cupola, thankful that he didn't have to ride with his head inside the awful-smelling vehicle. As the vehicle bumbled south, he checked the forged papers that were written up for him.

When he was satisfied everything was in order, he ducked down into the armored belly and spoke.

"Alright," said Mackinsky. "From here on in, we speak only German. Drive slow. If something looks off, I'll give the abort signal. 'Til then, play it cool."

Tanner took his grip off the steering wheel and gave a thumbs-up. Mackinsky stood up again and basked in the fresh air that swept across his face.

Near a little bend in the forest road, the BMP slowed to a crawl. Mackinsky scanned the area then signaled with a stomp of his foot. The rear hatch swung open and Manny rolled out the back. Bates reached over and clanged the door shut. Mackinsky could only hope that no one had seen a huge man run off into the bushes with an M21 sniper rifle.

Further along the road, the BMP reached a roadblock manned by three men carrying assault rifles. A machinegun nest sat to one side, and a T-55 tank on the other. Its main gun was pointed directly at them. Mackinsky's gut tightened at the thought of what might happen if things went wrong here.

The young officer at the checkpoint spoke in a clipped manner. His face betrayed no signs of friendliness or camaraderie. Each interrogative came in rapid-fire sequence. Mackinsky shot back each response without hesitation.

The cover story was simple. They had been sent back from the front by the commander of Panzer Regiment 17 to fetch a load of emergency supplies for its HQ.

Mackinsky talked up the dilapidated state of the BMP to help add an air of legitimacy to the story. His unit was in fierce combat with the Belgians and communications were no longer working. As a result, standard requests for resupply were just not getting through. In truth, the unit he was referring to had been wiped out less than 12 hours ago.

After a couple of minutes of checking the paperwork and signing forms, the duty officer signaled. One of the guards stepped into a booth and spoke on a field telephone. Thirty seconds later, the gate was raised and the BMP continued along the road.

Just beyond the trees sat the compound, hidden under the forest canopy. The entrance to the forest was marked by a pair of tracks cut into the tall grass. Once inside, Mackinsky ordered a halt near the north side of the open-air compound. Its neat rows of crates and supplies were lined up like some huge military-grade supermarket.

Tanner and Bates wandered off, their bags laden with explosives and detonators. Mackinsky went shopping for Major Brandt.

As he strolled down the wide aisle, he scanned the stenciled markings that indicated the contents of each box and crate on the shelves. There was everything here that a modern tank regiment might need – extra tracks, de-bogging beams, and field repair kits.

After some searching, Mackinsky found a crate of rifles – along with a surly captain who demanded to see the paperwork for his field requisitions. Mackinsky handed it over and watched the man's face fall. The captain stabbed a finger at the extra notation for small arms.

"This doesn't look official," he snarled.

Mackinsky shrugged. "It was a sudden change. Sorry. You know how colonels can get when they're in a hurry. It's a war, after all."

The captain flinched as if someone had just belched in his face.

"Well, that's not procedure," he said. An angry line creased his brow. "The paperwork should have been filled in again. You know that!"

Mackinsky kept cool and nodded along. This was not his first time facing a nit-pick bureaucrat. In fact, it was a relief to know that the other side had their fair share of them too. Besides knocking the guy out or shooting him, the only thing to do was to wait until the man released his pent-up anger and wandered off. That was how it worked back home too.

As the man's tongue wagged on, Mackinsky let his mind wander to the progress of his teammates. At this point, Manny would be in position and Tanner and Bates would no doubt have half the place wired to blow. When the verbal lashing ran its course and he had apologized and promised never to make such a grievous error ever again, the captain pursed his lips and marched off.

Mackinsky loaded two large boxes of East German rifles and 7.62mm ammunition into the back of the BMP. As he walked back for a final trip, he was sure that his troubles were over. They were not.

While holding a case of grenades, Mackinsky turned around to find the pesky East German captain once again. The officer curtly informed him that next time the paperwork needed to be filled out correctly or he would be denied his request.

"That makes sense," said Mackinsky.

The captain took a quick step back. It dawned on Mackinsky that he had just used the Anglicized form of the German phrase – something an East German would never have said.

The linguistic misstep marked him. Now there would be questions and phone calls and a load of contradictions that he couldn't explain.

The captain's hand shot out. "Let me see those papers again!"

Mackinsky threw the case of grenades at the East German. By instinct, the man raised his hands to catch it. Mackinsky's right hook shattered the captain's nose. A knee to the groin sent the East German to the floor in a bloody heap. Mackinsky stood over him like a prizefighter.

As he rubbed his sore knuckles. a squad of East German soldiers rushed around the corner with their weapons pointed in Mackinsky's direction.

HEY NOW

Mackinsky wrestled the pistol from the captain's holster and fired it at his pursuers. A stream of shots sprayed back in his direction as he sprinted down the long aisle. Upon rounding the corner, he found himself within arm's reach of a soldier who stood there with his mouth gaping open.

Mackinsky fired twice into the East German's chest. A chorus of angry shouts rose up behind him and he fled once again. A series of turns took him out of the maze of supply shelves toward the open area that dominated the center of the compound.

Mackinsky made a beeline toward the commander's office. Not even the sight of a T-55 tank at the nearby refueling station slowed his progress.

The tank's commander popped his head out of the hatch and screamed. Mackinsky watched in horror as the Russian lunged for the .50 caliber machinegun and drummed out a stream of high-caliber fire. The shots whisked over his head and smacked into the supply shelves. Mackinsky tossed a grenade at a clump of barrels near the tank and threw himself at the ground.

The searing heat bit at his flesh as a thundering explosion ripped through the compound. Flaming pieces of jagged metal sliced through the air. A sheet of flames engulfed the tank. It burned like some monstrous effigy.

Mackinsky got up and charged through the thick cloud of dark smoke. When he finally reached the scuffed metal door of the commander's office, he halted and listened.

Off near the perimeter of the depot, dribs and drabs of automatic rifle fire welled up into a cacophony of angry exchanges. Amid the chatter, Manny's sniper fire boomed out. Each of his shots cut down an enemy guard. Soon, the dull pop of Kalashnikovs dwindled.

Tanner and Bates emerged from behind the wreckage of a small collapsed shed and jogged toward Mackinsky. As both men approached, a foul odor made him gag. The source of the stench soon became apparent. Bates was covered from head to toe in crap.

"I told you not to wire up the latrines!" he shouted.

Tanner laughed and held up both hands in protest.

"We were ordered to torch this place and that's exactly what I'm doing."

"Enough," Mackinsky said. "We go in. We grab what we need. We get the hell out of here."

Bates slammed the butt of his rifle on the doorknob. Mackinsky kicked the door open and Tanner fired a short burst. The three men piled inside.

A dead East German officer lay on the ground in front of a massive wooden desk. Mackinsky snatched the stack of papers atop of it and stashed them in his pack. Back outside, dozens of East Germans scurried through the dense smoke. Ammunition stored on the north side of the compound popped off like long strings of firecrackers. Tanner pulled the trigger of the claymore detonator. A series of explosions hammered in the distance.

The three Americans ran along the fence until they reached the BMP. Manny sat inside with the barrel of his rifle poking through one of the rear firing ports. As Mackinsky scrambled inside, Manny squeezed off a round.

"Man, am I glad to see you guys," he said. "What's that smell?"

In the dim light of the Soviet armored personnel carrier, Tanner shuffled into the driver's seat while Bates sat in the gunner's position.

"Let's get the hell outta here!" Mackinsky yelled.

The BMP's engine awoke like an old man. Tanner shoved the pedal to the floor and the vehicle jerked forward.

"Enemy tank behind us!" Manny shouted.

Mackinsky peered through the vision block as the big tank's main gun flashed. A split second later came a deafening whoosh as the round sailed overhead. Fifty yards ahead of the BMP, a clump of trees shattered as a massive explosion tore into them.

"Move!" shouted Mackinsky. He balled his hands into fists and pounded hard on Tanner's back.

The BMP leaned to the right and turned off the forest path. The hull screeched like nails on a chalkboard as it scraped against the trunks of tall pine trees. The forest thinned and soon they were careening down a steep slope. Tanner cried out just as the vehicle plunged into gently flowing waters.

Torrents of water washed over the hull and gushed through the turret hatches. The flood pooled on the floor of the vehicle and Mackinsky's pant legs were soon soaked. Something was very wrong. Their vehicle was amphibious, wasn't it?

Mackinsky pushed back at the terror that welled up inside. What did he know about these things? BMPs had no snorkel or flotation devices. But they did have one critical piece of equipment that needed to be prepped before entering the water.

"The trim vane!" screamed Mackinsky. "Get up there and un-fold the trim vane!"

Manny shoved open the top hatch and crawled along the slick deck of the BMP. When he got to the front, he jammed his boots up against the long flat piece of metal folded against its front. After three swift kicks, the panel gave way. The current slid up against the trim vane and retreated. The vehicle righted itself and the hull front popped above the water's surface.

Mackinsky ducked back into the vehicle and patted Tanner on the back. The engine gurgled as he accelerated, and the BMP trundled toward the river's opposite bank. When they were no more than halfway across, a geyser of water shot up into the air twenty meters to their left.

"That T-55 is back!" Mackinsky shouted. It was perched near the crest of the slope behind them.

No doubt its 100mm main gun was busy being reloaded while the gunner adjusted his aim. If the BMP was still in the water when the big tank fired again, they were all as good as dead.

A shudder of relief swept along Mackinsky's spine as the vehicle's treads latched onto solid ground. The carrier dug into soft mud before it finally found its grip and started up the embankment.

Mackinsky flung open the commander's hatch and popped up just in time to see the T-55 fire again. This time, the round was close enough to whip fragments of dirt and rock against the BMP's bent armored skirts. Manny swung open the rear hatch and tossed out armfuls of smoke grenades. Their trail was soon covered by billowing clouds of yellow and red.

"Keep going!" shouted Mackinsky.

They sped off into the dark countryside. No more was heard from the pursuing enemy tank. Minutes later, Mackinsky ordered a halt at the edge of a field and checked his map.

He tapped Tanner on the shoulder and directed him north. The BMP halted near a copse of trees. Mackinsky noted the coordinates and jumped out.

"Why are we stopped?!" shouted Bates.

"Get all the supplies out of here now and cover it with a net," said Mackinsky. "Hurry!"

Crates and boxes were flung out the back of the BMP to land in a messy heap of waist-high vegetation. Mackinsky threw a moss-colored camouflage net over top and shrugged. It wasn't perfect, but it would have to do. If Brandt and his men could get here quick enough, they just might have a chance at finding the cache before the East German Army.

Back aboard the BMP, the four-man team continued its journey until they found the pavement of a nearby road. A few minutes later they stopped in the middle of a marshy area with tall reeds and pools of knee-deep water.

"That's it," declared Mackinsky. "We're on foot from here."

The team ran through the night until their lungs were ready to burst. Minutes later, the Blackhawk popped over the horizon and sped low towards them. The chopper skimmed along the ground. Each man jumped on board and they were off once again.

Over the din of the rotor, Manny glanced over at Mackinsky and smiled.

"That wasn't so bad now was it?" said Manny.

Twenty-five minutes later, they neared Wiesbaden Army Airfield just west of Frankfurt. Tanner pointed down at the blackened patch of ground just short of runway 26. The surrounding debris left no doubt as to its cause.

Ground crews rushed back and forth to fuel up long lines of NATO aircraft. A pair of A-10s touched down and halted short of the fresh concrete. The huge grey circle marked a hasty attempt to repair the damage caused by a Russian bomb.

The Blackhawk's wheels tapped the ground and the team disembarked. Colonel Evans sat ten yards away in his jeep. An expression of dread was stitched across his face. Without a word, everyone got in.

Evans threw the vehicle into gear and sped away from the helicopter as it lifted off once again, presumably on its way to another mission. The 62nd Aviation Company, aka "The Royal Coachman", had zero downtime since the start of the war. The pilots only landed their aircraft to rearm and refuel.

When Mackinsky and the rest of the team arrived at the little series of hutches on the north perimeter of the base, the other men jumped out.

Evans gripped Mackinsky's shoulder. Peter halted and faced the colonel. The lines on his face revealed long hours of frustration and grief. Mackinsky studied the man for a moment and realized that some fresh burden lingered behind those tired eyes.

"Peter," he said. "It's your dad. He's missing."

"You awake?"

Harland said nothing. Everything hurt. He kept his eyes clamped shut and tried to summon sleep's tender mercies. The whisper slid out toward him again.

"Yeah, you're awake."

Harland peered through a pair of swollen eyes. The world was a blurry haze of gray. An engine roared to life and a series of jolts sent fresh waves of pain along every inch of his body.

Was this a part of the torture that the Russians had devised for him? If so, he would tell them whatever they wanted – anything! All he wanted was a reprieve from this ceaseless suffering.

"You took one hell of a lickin'."

Harland recognized the grizzled voice. An ember of hope flickered somewhere deep inside. For a long moment, he nurtured its brittle warmth before parting his cracked lips to speak.

"Franklin?"

Both syllables sounded like crushing defeat. Harland scarcely believed the voice was his.

"Listen up, soldier. You gotta keep yourself together right now. The enemy's got a hold of you, and if you give up then you're a goner. Do what you need to do. Keep yourself alive. Find reasons to keep going."

Ridiculous. Harland couldn't see the point. The future was out of his hands. Soon, he would face torture and death at the hands of the enemy.

"Let me go," croaked Harland.

"Minute by minute," said Franklin. "That's the key. There's only now. Hold on, you hear? Hold on or you're lost."

Harland stood on the precipice of a despair that would swallow him whole. Behind him was Franklin with his hand outstretched. With tremendous effort, Harland took a single step back from the brink.

The truck stopped and the a gate creaked open. An angry voice bellowed in a foreign tongue.

"I can't stick around here anymore. Take care."

Before he could beg Franklin to stay, someone scooped up Harland and dragged him along the packed earth. His world filled with the shouts of furious men and the barks of angry dogs. He was dropped like a sack of potatoes. Someone poured a trickle of water down his throat. Harland dozed in a haze of agony and confusion.

***

When Harland awoke, it was daytime and his vision had cleared. He lay in a cot in the middle of a soccer pitch. A glance at his arm revealed that the tattered piece of dirty gauze from yesterday had been replaced by a fresh white bandage. Someone – he had no idea who – had apparently changed it overnight.

Harland spent the morning soaking in his new surroundings. There was no roof and the whole camp was open to the elements. Little puddles of rainwater dotted the grounds here and there. The grass on the pitch had been trampled into mud.

Russian soldiers armed with assault rifles and machine-guns looked down from tall guard towers. Prisoners of various nationalities huddled together in the stands. Some of them slept on the cold metal benches. Harland wasn't sure what had qualified him for a cot, but he was thankful for it. Maybe some sliver of compassion still remained in this world.

A commotion erupted as one of the prisoners limped toward the main gate. Someone screamed a warning. The man paid no heed. One of the guards in the nearest tower aimed his rifle and fired a long burst that raked the prisoner up and down. He collapsed face-down in the dirt. Blood pooled underneath the body. No one ran over to help.

Harland took some relief in what he had just witnessed. He now understood a foolproof method of giving up. But last night's conversation with Franklin had temporarily ruled that out. For now, he would search for a reason to stay alive. Perhaps if he could find a friend to help guide him through the coming hardships, things might be a little easier.

The only problem was that Harland had never been very good at making friends. He had always been a loner at school and even in the army. His former crew mates in *The Terminator* hadn't really socialized with him outside of their duties. It was nothing personal. Most of them were tough kids who boasted about stuff that never interested Harland much – drinking, partying, and getting all the girls.

The same old feeling of being an outsider took over as he observed the men around him. From the looks of their fatigues and the way they spoke, it was plain that he was surrounded by West Germans. A few clumsy attempts at making small talk ended in exchanges that never really went anywhere. Though the men he spoke with were unfailingly polite, it was plain to Harland that he was forcing them to speak in English – a language in which not all of them were fluent.

After ten minutes of chatting about mealtimes and where to get extra blankets, he retreated from the conversation and took from them a tendered pack of cigarettes. Harland recognized this immediately for what it was - a subtle reward for finally taking the hint and excusing himself.

Over toward the middle of the soccer pitch, Harland watched a group of Canadians doing jumping jacks and jogging in tight circles. The idea of joining them seemed ridiculous. Each time he breathed in just a little too much, it felt like someone was plunging a needle into his chest.

The skin on his arms and legs were black and blue and the little finger of his right hand was set at an unnatural angle. Unable to do much else, he rested.

IN ASKING LAND

12 km NE of Fulda

First Lieutenant Darren White jabbed a finger at the square plastic buttons on his commander's console and swore. Each inhalation brought with it the stale hot stink that permeated the belly of the tank. All he could think about was getting back out into cool fresh air. He had just about enough of playing around with the Abrams' fire control system.

"Try again," he growled.

Sergeant Torrence leaned over and looked through the primary gunner's sight.

"Anything?" asked White.

"Nope. Just black."

White slapped a gloved hand against his thigh.

"I need to check on some things," he said. "Keep on it. See if you can get it working again."

Outside the tank, the world came alive once more with the shriek of artillery rounds and rockets. The racket hadn't paused since the start of the war, but White barely noticed it now. Just like the chatter of a machinegun or the chronic case of constipation from eating MREs, the ceaseless drum of long-range fire had come to blend in with the banalities of daily life. It was strange how quickly people got used to things.

White's tired eyes wandered over the battle-scarred remnants of Fox Troop. Three M1 tanks and a platoon of Bradleys were all that was left of what had once been a company-sized force of the 2/11 Armored Cavalry Regiment. As part of Operation First Strike, the troop's men and vehicles had performed admirably. They had cleared the enemy defenses and seized their objectives ahead of schedule. After consolidating its hold on Objective King, Fox Troop had done as ordered and waited for the arrival of reinforcements from 8th Infantry Division.

Instead of being greeted by the sight of M60 Pattons, White and his men were attacked at point-blank range by a company of T-80s. The destruction of two M1 tanks was the first indication that the Russians had launched a counterattack. Only a tenacious close-range defense led by 2 Platoon's leader, Second Lieutenant Maurice Fitzgerald, had saved the entire company from certain death.

Colonel Mackinsky, the task force commander, had radioed for a general retreat, but Fox Troop was separated from the main body of Task Force Lance. Figuring that the battle had been lost, Fox dashed west toward the town of Lüdermünd in hopes of escaping along with the rest of the retreating task force. While heavily engaged with the Soviet force in pursuit of Bravo Company, a dozen NATO jets screeched overhead and dropped their ordnance on both the Russians and Fox Troop.

A ceaseless storm of napalm and iron bombs rained down on the men and vehicles. Anyone caught out in the open was instantly killed. When the hammerfalls ceased and the smoke finally withered, less than half of Fox remained. The troop's original commander was dead.

Of cold comfort was the fact that the Russians had suffered much worse – not a single Soviet vehicle or man near Lüdermünd stirred. White took command and rallied the shell-shocked survivors. They moved quickly, fearing more airstrikes would soon arrive. When they arrived near Lüdermünd, they found its bridge destroyed. With no way back home, the only option was to drive east - deeper into enemy territory.

White expected to be captured or killed immediately. Instead, the scouts had done an admirable job of finding the quickest and easiest route to cover, which turned out to be a giant patch of wooded hills to the southeast of their original objective. The Breitenbachtal Forest was a huge expanse of pine trees that covered nearly ten square kilometers. It was a perfect hiding spot.

The woods harbored a maze of deserted logging roads that no one had ever bothered to map out. The little folds and nooks of rolling woodland offered plenty of hiding spots for a small group of men and vehicles. A liberal application of combat netting and huge piles of thick branches had rendered Fox Troop invisible from the steady flow of air traffic above.

Despite such an ideal hideaway, the possibility of discovery loomed large. The prospects of keeping his tanks and armored personnel carriers hidden in enemy-occupied territory seemed daunting. Half of White's scouts were out there now, finding more hiding places big enough to conceal the men and vehicles.

Despite their recent ordeal, everyone in Fox Troop was in high spirits. Although they had taken appalling losses in Operation First Strike, most of them agreed that taking part in a counterattack was way more invigorating than the tactical retreats that characterized NATO's fighting strategy. It was no secret that American forces in the Fulda Gap were suffering mightily under constant blows from the Soviet 8th Guards Army.

Second Lieutenant Fitzgerald wandered over and stood before White. The young man's rugged good looks and narrow eyes lent him the mystique of a gunfighter sizing up an opponent on some dusty street in the old west. Truth be told, Fitzgerald was anything but the Clint Eastwood type. The kid had a brain that never stopped whirring along and spitting out new ideas. Word had it that the square-jawed second lieutenant sported a degree from some Ivy League college. If it was true, the guy had never brought it up.

White looked over at his newly minted second-in-command and mentally berated himself for not having tried harder to make acquaintances. Though they had trained and worked together sparingly for the last three months, both men ran in different circles and neither had made any real attempt at bonding during the countless regimental dinners and social functions that dotted a cavalry officer's schedule. Consequently, White had neither a good measure of the man nor a real appreciation of his abilities.

"Well," White said. "Whaddya figure?"

"Not good," said Fitzgerald. He gestured to the neat piles of crates and jerry cans that sat in the middle of the clearing. Tasked with accounting for and redistributing the troop's remaining supplies, the second lieutenant had taken to the job with a rare zeal.

"Just how bad is it?" asked White.

Fitzgerald read off his clipboard like a preacher giving a Sunday sermon.

"Casualties: Two of my scouts died on the way here. Third-degree burns. The bodies will be buried in twenty minutes. We have six WIA. One of them won't make it without a field hospital. The others are out of the fight – mostly broken limbs or burns. They need medical attention soon. All told, we have fifty more or less healthy men who can walk and shoot without any real problems."

"How's morale?" asked White.

Fitzgerald shook his head. "We lost a lot of men today. Everyone's grieving right now. That being said, most of them want payback against Ivan. Everyone wants to kill more Russians," he said.

"Let's have a quick service for the fallen," said White. "Just a few words. I want you to keep the men as busy as possible. Light duties for everyone else. Keep their minds and their hands occupied."

"Done," said Fitzgerald. He made a note and continued with the rundown of equipment and supplies.

"Fuel: Your three M1s are down to half a tank each. All three Bradleys are at one-quarter empty. Ammunition: Each of the tanks now has six rounds loaded in their ready racks. To be specific, that load consists of two sabots and four HE rounds. My scouts have four Dragons with two missiles each and half a dozen LAWs. For air defense, we have a grand total of two Stingers. The mortars are completely out of rounds but each of my four squads has a pair of M203s and a case of grenades. Food: Here's the big problem. We have enough for about two or three days – maybe four if we go half MREs. Canteens are low, but one of my guys found a stream about half-a-klick north of here."

"I guess we could always go hunting out here," said White.

Fitzgerald didn't crack a smile. White sensed the joke being computed in that big brain.

"I'll have the men set up some snares," said Fitzgerald. "But my major concern is the fuel situation. Sooner or later, we'll need to ditch those tanks."

A bolt of anger pushed White a step forward.

"You're not suggesting my crews pick up rifles and run around with you crunchies?"

"Sir, it's pretty hard to keep three tanks hidden from sight," said Fitzgerald.

"Agreed," said White. "The only problem is that the tanks are our only major source of firepower. Without armor support, we'll be sneaking around and running away from everything. We can't fight without tanks."

Fitzgerald's jaw dropped open.

"S-Sir…we are in no shape for a fight," he said. "The operation…has failed. We need to tell someone we're here and get back home. If we stay, we're dead. Do I need to mention that one of my – one of your men needs advanced medical attention?"

"I get all that. But we're also in a perfect position to hurt the Russians real bad," said White. "We're behind their lines and we have the advantage of both surprise and mobility. I just need your scouts to go out there and find targets -"

Fitzgerald put a hand up. "Sir, the first time we rear our heads, the Russians will have a whole tank regiment come down on us. While I understand and share your desire to engage the enemy, I can't go along with the idea of staying out here like some kind of Robin Hood."

"Let me be clear here. We're still at war," said White. "If there's an opportunity to deal some damage to the Russians without undue risk, we'll take it."

"For how long sir?" said Fitzgerald. "Even if we can do that, we'll run out of supplies. At some point, things are going to break."

"They're already breaking," admitted White. Grudgingly, the words came out. "My primary sight's gone. Gunner's using the AGS right now." The auxiliary gunner's sight was still useful for engaging enemy tanks but it required a lot more work for the tank's gunner to hit targets, especially on the move.

Fitzgerald folded his arms against his chest and said nothing. White dug at the ground with the tip of his combat boot.

"We can't repair that here," said Fitzgerald. "Our options are extremely limited."

"I know that," said White. "But what the hell good does knowing do?"

"This isn't easy for me either," said Fitzgerald. "Do you want analysis or commiseration?"

White pushed out a long breath.

"Mostly your analysis."

"We have three options. Number one - disband the unit and send everyone off to find their way home. Most of us will die or get captured. Two - we can stay here and fight like some kind of American version of the Viet Cong. We all die or get captured. Option three, we find a way to communicate with friendlies and arrange for a pickup. Everyone lives. I think that spells things out sufficiently. Sir."

White's eyes wandered up to a sky crisscrossed by a thousand cotton-like contrails. He had never imagined there were so many aircraft in the world until the war started. They were a constant presence over the battlefield. Early on, the men would stop what they were doing and witness a dogfight unfold above them and cheer as if they were watching a football game. White had put a stop to it after a while, but he suspected the guys were now bored of it anyway.

"There's plenty of friendly aircraft," said White. "We could radio someone. Airlift our wounded out of here. Get some supplies in."

Fitzgerald shook his head.

"Our vehicle radios are short range and can't access aircraft frequencies. Maybe if we had a command vehicle. Even then, you'd have to broadcast on a guard channel. Everyone and their mother would hear you."

"How about just waiting for an aircraft and popping a dozen yellow smoke grenades then?" said White. "We got plenty of those."

"Someone friendly might see it…but so would the enemy. Three guesses as to which of the two would get here first. Signaling at random aircraft with mirrors might work, but it's just as likely we'll catch the attention of a Soviet plane as an American one. Even so, the pilots are either flying way too high to see us, or way too low and fast. Those guys are focused a hundred percent on dodging terrain and enemy fire. Getting someone's attention from here is like trying to hitch a ride at the Indy 500."

White kicked at the hard ground, sending a clod of dirt flying in the direction of his Abrams tank. He now had an idea of who Lieutenant Fitzgerald was, and he did not like this man at all. White wanted solutions. Fitzgerald gave him problems.

"Well, you're no damn help at all, are you?" said White. "I send up an idea and you just shoot it down. What's your suggestion then, space cadet? Send a telegram?!"

A smile spread across Fitzgerald's face like butter on toast.

"How about…calling someone?"

White burst out laughing. "That is the dumbest thing I've ever heard," he said. "Go back to college."

Fitzgerald pressed on. "Have you picked up a phone since this conflict began?"

"The Russians would have cut the lines first thing," said White. "But to answer your question – no, I have not used a telephone recently. As you can tell, I've been a little busy. What makes you think the phones still work?"

"Redundancy," said Fitzgerald. "My father worked at Bell Labs for thirty years. Engineer. You know how those guys think? They plan for adversity – disasters and wars. He used to bring home these giant books full of government standards. They were as thick as that tree trunk over there! Which would you find harder to believe - the idea that the West German government never anticipated the effects of a war on their telecommunications network or that they never even bothered?"

White shrugged. "Well…they had four decades to think about it," he said.

"Exactly," said Fitzgerald. "And if there's one thing the Germans are known for, it's over-engineering." He then went on a tangent about how difficult it was to dismantle a telecommunications network short of nuclear attack. The whole system, Fitzgerald explained, was distributed and dispersed. White let his mind wander as the man lectured him about nodes and circuit switching and other stuff that he neither understood nor cared about. By the time Fitzgerald had finished, five very long minutes had passed.

"What the hell," said White. "It's worth trying just to confirm that it won't work."

Both men mulled over a map of the area and guessed at the most likely locations of payphones. There were plenty of gas stations and schools around. It seemed likely they would find at least one phone without too much effort. If that didn't work, they could try the houses. Most German homes had a telephone in them – but going into a populated area meant almost certainly encountering the Soviets too.

"Assuming this works," said Fitzgerald, "we need a code based on a point of reference that only our side can understand. There's a chance the Russians might listen in on what we have to say."

"Good thinking" said White. "It better be a strong one. We've got a lot of explaining to do."

"No. We're only going to reveal our identification and approximate location," said Fitzgerald. "The more we try to say, the more likely the code will be broken."

White shrugged. "Bible verses?"

"Too obvious," said Fitzgerald. He dug into his pocket and pulled out his notebook. The second lieutenant flipped through the pages and stopped suddenly. "Mackinsky used chess pieces as code names. Take a look at this map. What do you see?"

"First Strike," White said. "The operational plans. Spit it out, Fitzgerald. What are you getting at?"

"Fox Troop's call sign was Firefox, right?" said Fitzgerald. "That's not something the Russians are going to know - our side's radio transmissions were encrypted with those new radios. But our guys know the callsigns. Major Clifton was his S2. You remember? He was there in the initial briefing. He can piece it together.

We'll put a call through to 8th Infantry Division and identify ourselves with our callsign, Firefox."

White wondered if the phone idea was really going to work. It seemed doubtful but there were precious other options available besides surrender or death. Before he picked up a rifle and headed out into the wilderness like some kind of Vietnamese peasant, he would at least try to make an honest effort to contact headquarters. If Fitzgerald proved himself wrong in the process, at least he wouldn't have to deal with any more of the wonder kid's "brilliant ideas."

"So…uh…that might work," said White. "But how are you gonna tell them where we are? I don't want the Russians to dump a ton of HE on this position."

Fitzgerald grabbed a grease pencil and sketched a series of squares over the tactical map. By the time he was finished, it resembled a chess board that was oriented along Task Force Lance's planned advance and objectives. The king's starting position was marked at the same location as Objective King, roughly eight kilometers east of Lüdermünd.

"Each chess square is one square kilometer on the map," said Fitzgerald. "Clifton knows our king's starting location. He knows the other pieces too from the other objectives. Three right diagonal and two forward moves on this map board bring us to where we are now. Indicating our current approximate location can be done with the use of standard chess notation."

"Last time I checked," said White. "The Russians played chess too."

Fitzgerald smiled. "True. But it's pretty hard to win if you can't see the pieces."

"Brief the scouts," said White. "Operation E.T. is a go. Let's phone home."

DREAM OPERATOR

Sergeant Haight wiped the sweat off his brow and scanned the ruined gas station for signs of a payphone. All that remained of the building was a mangled structure with scorched walls and burst windows. The pumps had melted and were now just ruined heaps of charred metal that sizzled like steaks on a hot grill. Three lumps of useless plastic and metal marked the former location of the station's public telephones.

Haight would have cursed the Russians for the destruction, but he knew better. As soon as things had kicked off, the West Germans had methodically gone down a list of items to be sabotaged. Gas stations were at the very top of that list. It was Haight's guess that some Territorialheer unit had simply plopped a couple of grenades into the underground diesel storage area and called it a day before driving west. If the Soviets wanted to conquer Western Europe, they would have to do it with their own damn gasoline.

Haight slammed a palm into the dusty ground. Lieutenant White had ordered him and his men out here to risk their lives on the most idiotic of missions. Haight had been trained to find enemy defensive positions, locate advance elements of Russian tank divisions, and send back intelligence that would play a key role in determining his unit's fate in any given battle. No one had ever prepared him to run around in enemy-occupied territory in search of a public telephone.

The gas station in front of them was Second Lieutenant Fitzgerald's third suggestion. Just like the first two locations, the search had yielded nothing. The next site was miles away and that meant sneaking through enemy-infested hills and betting that they wouldn't be detected. So far, Haight and his men had been lucky. But as any scout knew, the more time they spent out here, the more likely they would get caught. When that happened, the game was over.

Haight breathed in deep through his nose, taking in the stink of sweat and burnt diesel that filled his lungs. A pair of Urals zoomed down Highway 7. It was too dangerous to be out here. White and Fitzgerald didn't understand that.

A soft nudge on his shoulder brought Haight's attention to his right. Private Thomas lay there, smothered in foliage among the thick hedges. Haight nodded in the direction of the leafy pile.

Thomas jabbed two fingers toward his eyes and gestured with a sideways palm to the north. Like a shining monolith, a solitary phone booth stood there beside the highway. A glance through the binoculars revealed its pristine condition.

For a long moment, Haight doubted his own senses. How had he missed that? Tunnel vision. Perhaps it was the numbing fatigue or maybe he was just getting older. Either way, there was his objective – a telephone! A pair of Russian jeeps came rushing along the road and Haight tensed as he waited for them to pass. When they were out of sight, he gawked at Thomas and drummed his fingers in the dirt.

The phone booth may as well have been on the moon. It was a football field away and there wasn't a single ounce of cover around it for thirty yards in any direction. If an enemy vehicle came along while he was inside, its occupants would notice. Trapped in a coffin-sized box, he would be a sitting duck with nowhere to run as the bullets smashed into the glass enclosure.

And yet, there it was – beckoning him like a siren to a lonesome sailor.

"Hell with it," Haight muttered. "We'll try this one and if it don't work, we're gone."

Haight slithered back to the objective rally point to find the rest of his men. A few wordless signals were enough to kick things into motion. Security teams were set up on his flank and rear with a light machinegun to cover his approach. From a tree-lined ditch, he observed the phone booth once again and took a deep breath.

Haight mentally rehearsed the actions in his head. He would dash forward, plunk the coins in the slot, and dial the phone number that Second Lieutenant Fitzgerald had scrawled on a Juicy Fruit wrapper. Simple.

He charged up out of the ditch and through the row of trees. As his legs pumped and his arms swung back and forth, he repeated a phrase to himself like a mantra.

"Thisiscrazy. Thisiscrazy. Thisiscrazy. Thisiscrazy."

By the time he arrived at the phone booth, his heart was pounding like a heavy metal drummer. Each ragged breath spilled out in rapid wheezes. Haight chided himself for ever starting to smoke, while at the same time desperately wishing for a cigarette.

He jammed three sweat-soaked coins into the slot. Over the sound of their metallic rattle came the groan of an engine in the distance. Haight's gut clenched like a vise as he glanced through the window. Off to the east, a convoy of trucks rumbled down a hill and turned onto the highway. A moment of stark indecision paralyzed him. Did he want to die here in the phone booth? Or would he prefer to catch a bullet as he sprinted away?

Haight recalled his father's advice. As a habitual troublemaker, it had served him well in both high school and the army.

People see what they want to see. When you're in over your head, just look busy and act like you're supposed to be there. Total confidence. That's the key.

Haight steadied his stance and lifted the receiver. The Russians were going to see a man in uniform checking a phone line. In their mind, he would be a linesman sent out to test the telecommunications system. If that didn't work, his men would just kill all of them. It was just too bad that he was directly in the line of fire of his own machinegun.

To his immense surprise, a dial tone warbled out of the handset. Haight dug into his breast pocket and pulled out the gum wrapper. The little slip of paper tumbled from his shaky grasp and plunged gracelessly toward the dirty floor. Haight studied the ground for its whereabouts and bent over to retrieve it.

The first truck rushed by. A sudden gust of wind snatched the wrapper from his reach. The next truck came rushing along. Haight snatched the paper off the ground just as the last one approached. Its driver gawked at him with a wide-eyed expression of bewilderment. Sergeant Haight waved.

When the trucks were past, he stood there and wondered what had just happened. A garbled noise spilled from the receiver, which hung listlessly on its cord. Haight picked it up and spoke.

"Uh. Hello?"

A short pause. More fractured voices. This time, Haight could at least discern that it was a woman talking. The little bits of syllables and consonants sounded German but he couldn't be sure.

"Can you please connect me to…uh…8th Infantry Division headquarters in Frankfurt? Oh! Can you reverse the charges?"

Silence. Haight waited. Terror gripped his sides as he imagined a thousand dark outcomes to this misadventure. The Russian truck drivers had seen him and radioed someone about him. Instead of a German operator, he had been speaking with some junior officer from the Soviet signals branch. They were tracing his location right now. Very soon, a well-aimed artillery barrage would wipe him out. He was going to die - and for what? For some crazy idea that was never going to work in the first place.

"I hate you Lieutenant White!" he shouted.

On the other end of the line spoke a voice that sounded very annoyed and more than a little bewildered.

"Huntley speaking. Who is this?!"

Haight cleared his throat and shot out the words he had rehearsed a thousand times on the way here.

"I have a priority message for Major D.A. Clifton. This is Firefox. Repeat. This is Firefox. King is at G6. Repeat. King to G6. Message Ends."

Haight hung up the phone and sprinted back to his squad's position. They gathered up their equipment and zig-zagged south in an effort to shake any pursuers. Ninety minutes later, they returned to Fox Troop's hidden basecamp.

As he unscrewed the lid of his canteen, a helicopter's blades hacked at the air. Haight's heart banged furiously inside his chest and he imagined the worst. They had been followed back here and now a Hind was on the way to destroy them all. He got up to run and made it nearly halfway across the clearing when he noticed the distinct clatter of a Huey's rotors.

From the top of the nearest hill came an almost imperceptible flash of light from where B squad was positioned. The din of the Huey receded in the distance. Haight upturned the canteen and let its contents pour over his sweat-slick face and down his throat. Plain old water never tasted so good.

FOUND A JOB

Harland watched as the main gate swung open and a Russian officer strode through the entrance like a Roman emperor. He puffed out his chest, looked around at the crowd of prisoners, and hoisted a megaphone. Heavily accented words spoken in halting English swept out from its tinny speaker.

"Volunteer! Medical! Show hands!"

Silence descended over the camp like a curtain. No one moved. Harland had no idea what was being offered, but it had to be better than waiting to die. His hand went up and a guard snatched him by the arm and shoved him through the gate. Two other prisoners joined him. The men were pushed into the back of a huge military truck and the vehicle shot off into town.

As they rode along the deserted streets, Harland spied his surroundings. Men and tanks were scattered along the cobblestone roads at the center of the sleepy little burg. Several anti-aircraft vehicles dominated the town square. On the wider streets, Soviet soldiers ran back and forth along the sidewalks that were lined by little shops. All of the stores were shuttered – perhaps forever. It was obvious from the models of the abandoned cars that he was still in West Germany. A smirk crept across his face. Perhaps there was still a chance he would make it back home.

Harland spotted a sign in the roadway, bent over at forty-five degrees and punched full of bullet holes.

Hünfeld, it read. He had never heard of the place. The vehicle wound through the narrow streets and halted in front of a cream-colored four-story building with a red cross hung out front.

The tailgate swung open. Harland and the other prisoners in the truck were herded toward the hospital. Walking inside was like wading into a sea of suffering. Shattered young bodies in shredded khaki lay on the blood-soaked floors.

Doctors and nurses shuffled back and forth among the wounded. Upon their faces were etched stunned looks of helplessness and mind-numbing fatigue. Sickening howls of agony filled the corridors. The foul stench of body fluids was like nothing Harland had ever smelled in his life. Sour bile filled up within his throat and it was only due to the meager rations of the prison camp that he did not vomit. For once, he was thankful for an empty stomach.

A heavyset woman in a blood-smeared smock strode over to them. Her weathered face was expressionless. The way she spoke was robotic.

"Doctor or medic?"

Harland shook his head.

"I could use someone to look at my arm," he said.

She paused as if she were processing an equation that did not compute. After blinking twice, she spoke again.

"No. I am asking again. Are YOU doctor or medic?"

Harland wondered what a misunderstanding might cost him. He did not want to go back to the prison camp. On the other hand, he wasn't sure he wanted to stay here. In the end, he decided to go with honesty.

"Neither," he said. "I'm a tanker."

"If you tell me that, you must go back to the prison," she said. "We only have use for doctors or medics here. I will ask again. Are you a doctor? Or a medic?"

Harland scanned the sea of misery and weighed his choices. This place was a close second to Hell, but at least he would have something to keep him busy and take his mind off his own situation.

"Medic," he said.

The woman gave him a slow nod. Was there a glint of compassion in those eyes? It had been so long since anyone showed him any.

"You will not fit down here," she said. "The Russian doctors need an assistant. Third floor. Surgical ward. Go immediately."

Harland didn't budge. He knew only first aid and CPR. Working in a surgical ward seemed far beyond his meager abilities. And what was this about Russian doctors? Someone was either deeply confused or grossly overconfident in Harland's medical skills.

"Sorry, ma'am," he said. "But I think there's some kind of misunderstanding."

The doctor ignored him. She turned her attention to the two other prisoners with whom he had come here. After a few words they hurried off with her down the hall. Standing there alone, Harland looked back at the hospital entrance and considered the guards outside with their assault rifles. There was no chance of escape. The only thing left to do was go to work.

Harland trudged up two flights of stairs and swung open the heavy door. Conditions here were luxurious compared to the chaotic mess on the ground floor. There were beds for each patient and several of them appeared to have their own room. Harland could only guess at the reasons for the better treatment, and decided this floor was probably reserved for officers. The egalitarian principles espoused as central to the Soviet system apparently did not apply to the sick and wounded.

Harland ducked a head into one of the rooms where a pair of German nurses argued vehemently with a man in Soviet fatigues. Harland couldn't understand the nature of the bickering. Just before he turned to leave, the Russian unholstered a pistol and aimed it at the two young ladies.

Everything suddenly went quiet.

Harland limped off down the hallway. A shot rang out behind him. An inhuman scream followed. He wobbled onward and passed through a set of double doors that led back to the stairwell.

The world spun and he collapsed on the cold tiled floor. Harland curled into a ball. Rivers of cold sweat flowed over his body and soaked him to the bone. Shivers raced along his spine as though he'd been immersed in ice water.

Somebody wailed long and low. Harland realized the infernal sounds came from him.

There was no escape. This was Hell. It had to be.

He looked up to find an old man's face staring back at him. Harland tried to speak but only a dry croak pushed out of his mouth. Something sharp jabbed into his arm. The face dimmed until there was nothing at all.

STAY UP LATE

Peter Mackinsky fired off three quick shots, missing twice and hitting with the final one. His target tumbled backward and landed on the wooden floor without so much as a peep. Two other targets popped up and he squeezed the trigger once again before ducking behind the cover of a scratched metal desk.

The door at the other end of the room swung open so hard that the bottom hinges snapped off. Manny charged into the room, followed by Tanner and Bates. All three of them placed rounds into the rest of the enemies. A loud buzzer sounded and the kill house lit up in orange fluorescence. Mackinsky stood up and checked his watch.

"Thirty four seconds," he said. "Not a record. But not too bad."

Bates pointed to the room's entrance. The door leaned at an acute angle, as if it were bowing politely to the opposite wall.

"Nice one, Manny," he said. Maybe go easy on the John Wayne next time?"

The team walked together in file through the dusty rooms. The floor was littered in mangled paper targets.

"I appreciate your guys doing this for me," said Mackinsky. "You really should be resting up though. Especially after that last mission."

"Hey man," said Manny. "Don't worry about it. Times are tough. We're here for you."

The team fell silent at the clackclackclack of hurried footsteps. Evans tore into the room.

"Briefing room," said the colonel. "Now."

***

Evans held up a cassette tape in his hand and grimaced.

"What you're about to hear is a call made earlier today from a phone booth about ten kilometers north of Fulda. It's been cleaned up by sound technicians."

Evans slid the tape in and pressed play. A warbled series of sounds emerged from the speakers. A ringtone blared and then came two sharp cracks. The flow of words burst forth in rapid-fire succession. The voice sounded very far away, as if they came from the bottom of a well.

"…Major D.A. Clifton. This…FIREFOX. This…King *crackle* G6. Repeat…to G6…"

When the recording stopped, Evans played it one more time.

"It's meaningless without the right context," he said. "But when the message was passed on to Major Clifton, he understood immediately."

Mackinsky inhaled a sharp breath. Dennis Clifton was his father's intelligence officer. The two men had been good friends since they had arrived over here in Europe four years ago. Both of them had worked like mules to help meet and exceed the new standards that the army had put into place. If Clifton was involved in this, then maybe there were some answers about his father too.

"FIREFOX was the radio callsign for Fox Troop, which was assigned Objective King during the initial phase of Operation First Strike," said Evans. "The last half of the message was a puzzle but Clifton finally worked it out for our benefit. It's standard chess notation and indicates a location to the southeast of Objective King. About five kilometers."

Evans pointed to a map on the wall and indicated a heavily forested area to the north of Fulda. The entire area near the border was marked off in red to indicate its capture by the Russians.

Mackinsky leaned forward in his chair. He knew already what this was about. His father was out there with his men. He was alive and behind enemy lines. All they needed to do was go out there with a helicopter and pick them up. As if Evans could read his mind, the colonel cleared his throat and spoke up.

"There is no confirmation that this message is genuine," he said. "In fact, there's a decent chance that the Russians sent the message to lure in a rescue force. The fact that they hadn't completely dismantled the phone system behind their lines might be a deliberate attempt to use it for monitoring communications or planting false information to confuse us."

Evans stared at Peter as he continued speaking.

"We have to be very skeptical and extremely cautious about the conclusions we draw from this."

"Has there been any further contact?" asked Tanner.

Evans grunted. "We sent a Huey out there to sniff around an hour ago. It made visual contact with what appeared to be friendlies. We now know their exact location."

Bates folded his arms. "Why not land and check it out? They were right there!"

"Too much heat," replied Evans. "An air defense regiment has set up shop near Highway 7. Something big is happening over in that area. We can't get our planes too close or they'll get shot down. We've already lost an A-10 and a pair of F-16s in that sector."

"How are we going to mount a rescue operation then?" asked Bates.

"We are not going to rescue these men," said Evans.

"Huh?!" shouted Bates.

Mackinsky pushed his chair back and stood. Manny's hand clamped down on his shoulder and guided him down to his seat. The big man nodded and pointed toward Evans to continue.

"Your job is to go in there and contact these men. Assess what resources are available to them and determine who is still able to carry on operating in the area. Anyone wounded will be moved out of the danger area for a medevac."

Manny cleared his throat and raised a hand.

"You want eyes on the ground. Is that what you're saying?" he asked.

"I want them to conduct reconnaissance and, if necessary, combat operations in the enemy's rear," said Evans. "We need a complete picture of what Ivan is doing back there near Fulda. Photos taken from a recon aircraft or a satellite can only reveal so much."

"And our role is to babysit them?" said Bates.

"You'll be supporting them," said Evans. "I need you to set up a communications relay to the west of their location. You'll pass on their intelligence to us and feed them what we know."

Evans pointed to a large green box in the corner of the room. It was covered with knobs and buttons that made it look as if it belonged on a submarine or a jet airliner.

"This is a digital radio. The SEM-90," he said. "It's West German and it's about the best thing we have right now in terms of both power and encryption. It uses frequency-hopping technology that makes it damn near impossible for the enemy to eavesdrop on our communications. These were in the prototype stage when the war began. The few units we had ready were installed in Task Force Lance's vehicles right before Operation First Strike. The STA-80 fixed antennas should boost their range far enough to keep them in contact with your team. You'll need one for yourselves too."

Tannner tapped at his notepad with a pen and swiveled left and right in his chair like a kid going to the barbershop for the first time.

"So let me get this straight, sir," he said. "We contact FIREFOX. We confirm their situation and deliver the antenna. Then we come back west and set up a relay station? What if we get out there and find two guys and a peashooter?"

Evans set his hands on his hips. "You'll have to work with whatever you can get. We have zero support from above on this. Zero."

After discussing the details of the insertion and coordinating roles within the team, Mackinsky and his men filed out of the room. For the first time, he felt a sliver of hope at the prospect of seeing his father again. At the very least, if these men were under his command, they might know of his whereabouts or condition.

As the team walked outside toward the armory, a pair of jets screamed down the runway and took off. The roar of engines was enough to blot out all attempts at conversation. When they reached the underground bunker that served as the unit's weapons stores, Manny cornered Mackinsky as the other two men walked on.

"Pete, you okay with this one?" he asked.

"Manny, if you got my back then I'm all right," Mackinsky said. "You know it."

Nothing more needed to be said.

THE OVERLOAD

Harland woke up alone in a hospital bed that sat in the center of a large sterile room with white walls. A small table next to him held a steel tray that sported a number of sharp steel instruments lined up in a neat row. It wasn't hard to imagine the pain and horror the gleaming scalpels and saws could inflict on a human body. The realization of where he was and what was about to happen enveloped him with horror. He grunted and shook his head as his jaw trembled.

He summoned all his strength in an effort to bolt upright. A pair of leather restraints held him down to the stretcher. He yanked and cursed and gritted his teeth, but the straps kept him secure. Deep breaths helped to slow his racing mind.

Escape was possible. If he could just work his way out of the restraints, he would be home free. Grab a scalpel. Use it to stab the son of a gun who was guarding him outside the room. Secure his rifle then hijack a vehicle. Sure, why not?

Harland worked his hands back and forth in an attempt to wiggle out of the tight loops. Minutes spent pulling and twisting his wrists and bunching his fingers together resulted in no progress whatsoever. The bindings were fastened too tight and offered no avenue for escape. Harland stopped struggling and admitted to himself that he was trapped. A black sensation flooded through him as the last blossoms of hope withered and died.

The door swung open and a figure wearing a blood-smeared smock stalked toward him. The surgical mask covered the man's face in a way that smothered his humanity. Soon enough, this ghastly figure would wrap a hand around one of the sharp instruments and dig into Harland without mercy. It was all happening now. Dear God! He should have been more careful with the people in his life. His conscience brimmed with regret for every cruel word he had ever uttered.

"I'll talk," said Harland. He had meant to sound strong, but the words were a whimper.

The doctor lowered his mask, revealing a thin haggard face with high cheek bones dotted with graying stubble.

"Relax," he said. "I'm not here to hurt you."

His accent reminded Harland of the Imperial officers in Star Wars. It was a stereotypical "bad guy British accent." Something about it made American viewers want to root against those who spoke with it. Harland took a moment to wonder whether or not this was all a nightmare. If so, it was very convincing. The straps bit painfully into his wrists and ankles in a way that seemed anything but dreamlike. Still, there was something so bizarre about this situation that he had missed entirely the substance of what the man had just said.

"Sorry. What?" asked Harland.

"I said you should relax. Are you feeling any better?"

The doctor rolled the tray away from the bed and loosened the wrist straps. Harland rubbed his hands together as the flow of blood resumed to his fingers and the feelings returned. It was only then that he noticed his right pinky had been realigned and bandaged with a splint to set the broken bones. This time, there was no question of who had helped him. The man in the smock smiled and gestured toward Harland's finger.

"I'm…okay," said Harland. "What happened? Where am I?"

"Shhh. All that in good time."

The doctor set two fingers across Harland's wrist and counted quietly to himself while watching the clock on the wall. When fifteen seconds had passed, he nodded and smiled.

"You gave us quite a shock back there," said the doctor. "I can't have my assistant go into a panic, now can I?"

Assistant. Was this guy for real? And yet, Harland had been sent up here for a reason.

"Someone told me to come up here and help out the Russian doctors," said Harland. "Was that you?"

"You can change a bandage? Empty a bedpan?" asked the doctor.

Harland glanced over at the sharp surgical equipment. "Absolutely," he said.

"Then you'll do."

"Wait a second," said Harland. "Who are you? What is this place?"

"I'm Russian," said the doctor. "Ah, yes. I see you are surprised. I don't speak like the Russians in your American movies. Da comrade. We drink wodka, nyet? I went to medical school for many years in England before…this."

Harland stared in disbelief. This was the first time he'd ever met an Ivan in his life. The guy looked and sounded completely different from how Russians were portrayed in the comics and movies. With his easy smile and graying hair, the doctor seemed more like someone's grandpa.

"I am Doctor Kashuba. A surgeon by profession. You may call me Dmitri. I am aware you Americans prefer to keep things casual."

"How do I get out of here?" asked Harland. "You've got to help me."

Dmitri tsked.

"That attitude's only going to get the both of us in trouble. If you wish to venture an escape then I'm afraid you're on your own. You see, I am here as a member of the Soviet military and part of the ongoing operations being conducted against the Western democratic countries. If I were to assist you in such efforts, I would be arrested and killed for treason. And rightly so."

Harland slid down from the bed and hobbled around the room. His head swam at first but soon he was walking with no special effort. So many questions sprinted through his mind.

"Why are you helping me?" asked Harland. "What is this place?"

Dmitri put a hand up.

"This hospital has been liberated by our side. The ground floor is for Soviet enlisted men. The first and second floors are for our officers. You were on the second floor when I found you. I assume you meant to come up here and got confused by the different numbering system for these buildings."

Harland rolled his eyes at his own error. In Europe, buildings started counting floors after the ground floor. In his dazed and shell-shocked state, he had forgotten all about the difference with American buildings and had counted the ground floor as the first floor. What a stupid mistake!

"Here is the top floor – the third floor. Surgery and post-operative care. And I am not helping you at all. You are, in fact, helping me. I have a surgery scheduled here in less than an hour. Very important man, I am told. I expect you to help monitor the patient after I am finished. I need vitals taken every ten minutes and you will inform me immediately if anything is unusual."

Dmitri handed Harland a medical records sheet with the Russian words crossed out and the English terms scrawled just above them. It was easy to understand and Harland knew how to measure most of them – heart rate, breathing, blood pressure, and so on. A surge of confidence rushed through him.

"Sure," said Harland. "I can do this."

"Then do it well," said Dmitri. "Our lives depend on it."

TENTATIVE DECISIONS

Second Lieutenant Fitzgerald gazed up at the pink and purple pastels that slathered the western skies. He took a small amount of solace in knowing that despite all the death and destruction going on in the world, there were still beautiful sunsets. Back in New York, he had never really taken the time to enjoy moments like these, but that was a lifetime away. He was younger then and had taken the world and its splendor for granted.

As he wandered through the meadow where the men sat cleaning their weapons and packing their bags, he folded his arms together and wondered how many more days like this he might see. The world was at war now, and the unspoken thought on everyone's mind was how much longer things would go on until it went nuclear.

It was funny how nobody talked about that – almost as if doing so would invite it to happen. Like the rest of his men, he had watched "The Day After" on network TV a couple of years ago and spent the rest of the evening in a quiet haze. Unlike most, he hadn't forgotten it so easily. Instead, he spent the next several months devouring every last book he could read about the subject. The same amount of time was required to get over his subsequent depression.

Fitzgerald was filled to the brim with the cold bitter facts about what awaited. The countless photos of Hiroshima's scarred survivors could never be banished from his mind.

He recalled the projections of nuclear winter and the predictions of mass starvation that would kill off millions of irradiated survivors. Despite that knowledge, Fitzgerald was powerless to stop any of it from happening. None of it would matter when the bombs hit.

That prospect didn't seem to concern White. The man never broached the subject and dismissed all attempts to talk about the issue. Instead, he had just sat back and enjoyed the wild ride of being here behind enemy lines. Although Fitzgerald would never have admitted it, he too found it thrilling. By rights, the two men should never have gotten along due to their massive personality differences. The commander was a straight shooter without Fitzgerald's subtlety or penchant for overanalyzing. To put it another way, White was AC/DC to Fitzgerald's Talking Heads.

Despite being petrified of nuclear war, Fitzgerald was enjoying the intellectual challenges of being here. Merely finding a phone had been enough to distract him from the nightmarish images of mushroom clouds and radiation burns that danced in his head all day and night. Soon they would be rescued, and Fitzgerald wasn't sure how he was going to deal with that.

He had considered blowing his brains out. Two of his scouts had done just that when the war began, perhaps having decided that it was just easier that way than waiting for the inevitable. It was evident from the reports of riots and sporadic acts of violence back home that many people felt the same.

The whole world teetered on the edge of madness right now, just a nail head's breadth away from leaping into the void. His fingertips dragged back and forth along the butt of his holstered pistol. It would be so simple to just give in…

Fitzgerald yanked his hand back as if he just received an electric shock.

No. At least not right now.

He scanned the skies again and hoped for the thousandth time that the helicopters being sent to pick them up might be delayed for another day – maybe two.

Lacking a problem to focus his mind upon, the twilight descended upon him like a slowly closing curtain.

Soon it would be night again and he would struggle to keep his mind busy in an attempt to avoid sleep. The same recurring dream was there waiting for him in the darkness.

It went like this:

Fitzgerald would be walking along the gritty shops and restaurants of Hell's Kitchen minding his own business. Suddenly, there would be a brain-numbing flash. The red roiling mushroom cloud would rise up like some gigantic demon emerging from its ancient slumber. It towered over the skyscrapers of Midtown Manhattan, making them look tiny in comparison.

Before he could turn to run, the waves of flaming death would roll down the avenues and engulf the buildings like matchsticks. Fitzgerald would scream just before the wall of heat turned his bones to ash.

In the instant before he perished, his mind would fill with the knowledge that all trace of him and everyone he had ever loved would disappear. Every beautiful painting would be destroyed. Man's most brilliant achievements and discoveries would be turned to cinders. Every brave act against brutality and prejudice and blind hatred would be rendered null and pointless.

Fitzgerald despaired the raw violation of sense and compassion upon which such an act was predicated. It went against everything for which he stood.

His train of dark thoughts was derailed as a commotion erupted near the edge of the clearing. Fitzgerald caught a flash of movement near the tree line accompanied by whispers and low angry voices. After motioning for one of his scouts to wake up White, Fitzgerald walked over to investigate. Someone shone a hooded flashlight in the direction of the noise. The faint outline of several figures appeared in its muted beam.

Three scouts pointed their rifles at a group of captives, all four of whom wore American combat fatigues and helmets. Each man was laden with heavy packs. One of the prisoners carried a two-meter long pole across his broad shoulders.

"Report," demanded Fitzgerald.

Sergeant Haight stepped forward. He flipped up the bulky set of night vision goggles and spoke in a gravelly voice that seemed to be magically bestowed upon every man who wore three stripes on his sleeve.

"Sir, we caught these four men at the perimeter ten minutes ago. Our sentry challenged them. They failed to give the correct password. We took their weapons, bound their hands, and brought them here. They claim to be Americans."

Fitzgerald scanned the faces of the captives, but it was hard to discern much in the darkness. He wanted to believe these men were Americans, but caution was necessary. It was entirely possible the Soviets were looking for them and his scouts had found a razved-ka team. The briefings indicated that they commonly operated in such a manner, decked out in American gear and speaking flawless English to blend in.

"Who's in charge?" Fitzgerald asked.

The man in front stepped forward. The dim light caught his slim angular features. He was built like a quarterback and each subtle movement was smooth and confident.

"I'm Captain Peter Mackinsky," he said. "We came to make contact with you."

Fitzgerald looked over at Haight and raised an eyebrow.

"Sorry. Did you say Mackinsky?" said Fitzgerald. "Any relation to-"

"Colonel Ted Mackinsky?" said Peter. "I'm his son. Is he here? What happened to him?"

"Before I tell you that, I need to know you're who you say you are," said Fitzgerald.

"You want me to prove we're Americans?" said Mackinsky. "Let's see…the Tigers won the World Series last year. New Coke sucks. Bobby shot J.R. Now either shoot me or let me pass. I'm tired and this crap weighs a ton."

Fitzgerald rolled his eyes. The resemblance should have been enough. Peter Mackinsky was a younger and leaner version of his father. It was obvious this was no trick.

"Good enough," said Fitzgerald. "By the way, Kristin did it. Bobby was innocent."

Fitzgerald gestured to his scouts to unbind their hands but did not clear them to return the group's weapons. The four men didn't seem to care. They tossed their bags on the ground and collapsed in a heap on top of them.

"I haven't seen nor heard from Colonel Mackinsky since the Soviets counterattacked east of Lüdermünd," said Fitzgerald. "He called for everyone to retreat and then warned us of an incoming airstrike. That's the last we heard from him before we were forced to disengage and drive here. I presumed he had made it back with the rest of his men."

"Well, you know what they say about 'presume,'" said Mackinsky. "It makes a prez out of you and me."

White's irritable twang sliced through the night.

"Lieutenant Fitzgerald. Where the hell are you?!"

Fitzgerald aimed the hooded flashlight in the direction of the man's voice and flashed it three times. White stormed over in the darkness like an elephant stomping through a cornfield. Fitzgerald cringed as he listened to the man traipse toward them, cursing and mumbling the whole way. It was almost like White was physically incapable of being quiet. When the lieutenant arrived, he grabbed the flashlight and shone it in the faces of their newly arrived guests.

"I'm in command here. Who are you? What's all this about?"

Mackinsky didn't bother getting up. He tossed a hand toward White as though in greeting and introduced himself. White stepped back when he heard that he was speaking with a captain. Without prompting, he confirmed what Fitzgerald had already told him about Ted Mackinsky. No one knew a thing about him. White ordered the group's weapons returned and canteens full of cold water were produced.

Mackinsky explained the purpose of their visit and the orders to conduct operations in the surrounding area. White sounded ecstatic. He had wanted to stay here and fight, and now he had the official go-ahead to do just that. Fitzgerald was relieved at the news for his own reasons. Conducting a guerilla war in enemy territory sounded like just the project he needed to keep his mind focused on things other than the inevitability of nuclear annihilation.

"How's the war going?" asked White.

"Badly," said Mackinsky. "The Soviets are rolling us up. Give me a sitrep."

"We've found a couple of targets to hit out there already," said White. "Just give me some ammo and fuel for the tanks and-."

"No," snapped Mackinsky. "We don't want you carrying out combat operations yet. Your little phone call already stirred things up enough already. They know you're out here somewhere and there are search teams operating to the east."

Fitzgerald stared at the ground as his pride sunk to a new low. The phone had seemed like such a clever idea at first.

"What do you need us to do?" Fitzgerald murmured.

"We need eyes out there to collect information and relay it back to us," said Mackinsky. "Do not engage the enemy. Not yet. The whole point is to operate in a covert manner."

White's tone darkened at the news.

"Sir, I've got the best men in the world here," he said. "You let us off the leash and we'll raise so much Hell here that Ivan's gonna be sorry he ever thought of coming over that border."

"Lieutenant, I'll be ten kilometers to the west of you sitting at a relay station and listening to your hillbilly twang," said Mackinsky. "If I so much as hear a shot fired in anger, we're pulling each and every one of you out. You're to carry out my orders to the letter or I shut the whole operation down. If that's a problem for you, let me know. I'll have you brought out on a Blackhawk with your wounded."

While White backpedaled and tried to hide his obvious disappointment, Fitzgerald was elated about the mission. The thought of gathering intelligence seemed to be filled with exciting challenges. It would take every ounce of nerve to stay and operate right here in the bear's den. Success would depend on both tact and guile – two things which White would need to learn if they were going to survive.

"When do we get to work?" asked White.

"You're on the job now," said Mackinsky. "It's dark. Get your men out and moving around. We don't want to reveal your position with a medevac, so we'll carry your wounded back west to a PZ and have them airlifted out of here.

Write down a list of whatever supplies you need. Only the essentials. I'll bring it tomorrow. Let's arrange a password so I don't get shot."

Fitzgerald brought the map out and shined the flashlight on it. Mackinsky strolled over and pointed to the strip of Highway 7 that ran north to south near their current location.

"Ivan's been moving SAMs and AAA into this area recently," said the captain. "We're particularly interested in what's going on in this vicinity."

White sat in a sulking silence.

"We'll have a team out there right away," said Fitzgerald. "Expect a radio report by first light."

Mackinsky let a weary smile cross his face and nodded. Without further fanfare, the wounded were put on litters and handed to the four-man team. Five minutes later, they had disappeared back into the thick maze of forest. Fitzgerald assembled his scouts and gave a short briefing. Ten minutes later, all the teams were gone.

That night, Fitzgerald slept like a log.

The operating room door burst open, jolting Harland awake. Dmitri and another doctor emerged with a small team of nurses in tow. They spoke in very fast Russian to one another. One of the portly nurses pointed to him and snarled in an accusatory tone. The whole team paused and looked over at Dmitri.

The old man said something that made the nurse storm off while the others laughed uproariously. Harland couldn't shake the feeling that his right to be here had just been asserted. The whole scene could have come straight out of a M*A*S*H episode.

As the others shuffled off, Dmitri plopped down beside Harland and sighed as he rubbed at his temples. Deep lines of fatigue were etched into Dmitri's face. Suddenly, he was not just old, but ancient. Harland wondered at the man's age. Sixty? No way. Seventy-five seemed to be in the ballpark.

"How did it go in there?" asked Harland.

"He's alive," said Dmitri. "This was his third operation. The man should be dead. But! He's a fighter."

Harland had to wonder what all the fuss was about. Men were dying by the truckload on the first floor. Little had been done for them except bandage up whoever could be saved. The rest were left to die. And yet, Dmitri was up here with a surgical team, modern equipment, and a generator.

"What makes this one so important?" asked Harland.

Dmitri shook his head and gulped down water from a paper cup.

"A colonel. American."

Harland's gut roiled. Was he talking about Mackinsky?

"Colonel Who?"

The doctor stood up and stretched his long limbs. His reedy fingers interlaced and flexed together like a pianist preparing for a recital.

"Valuable prisoners are sent here and we save them. Once stabilized, they are sent east. I suppose for interrogation."

Harland shot up. "Is that what happens to the prisoners over at the camp?"

Dmitri cracked his knuckles then rotated his neck in wide circles.

"I'm sure I don't know what you are talking about. Come, let me show you how to maintain an IV."

Harland's gut churned. This man whom he had once thought of as a noble saver of lives was only part of a factory-like process that led to some torture chamber. A chill wind blew through Harland's soul. This was no father figure. He was looking at a monster. Harland jabbed a finger at Dmitri and snarled.

"The enlisted men. What happens? Tell me."

Dmitri slouched over and gazed at the ground. He looked like an old man. When he spoke, the words were nudged out by a fumbling conscience.

"I honestly don't know, Will. Asking questions like that is dangerous. But if I knew, I would tell you. I do my job here. If not, they kill me. I just want to do what I'm told so I can go back…see my grandchildren."

Harland thought for a minute. He should have known better than to take any comfort that he might help someone. The patients here were being helped only enough to prepare them for the shock of torture after they were well enough. The whole lousy operation was built on the most cynical of foundations.

He wanted so badly to quit but it was clear enough that nothing would be accomplished by doing so.

Dmitri would simply ask for another volunteer and someone else would be up here caring for patients. Harland would go back to the prison or be shipped off to some work camp to die.

"It seems like I have no choice," said Harland. "Give me the stethoscope."

The edges of Dmitri's mouth budged upward and Harland couldn't help but feel he had just made a deal with the devil.

"The patient is right over there," said the doctor. "Check vitals every fifteen. If there's anything irregular, I want you to wake me up immediately."

***

Harland's heart hammered in his chest as his eyes wandered over the patient. He was a great big bear of a man. The colonel's face was bandaged, but Harland already knew his identity. The stocky frame belonged to none other than Colonel Ted Mackinsky. Fate had brought them together once again.

Harland held up a meaty wrist and took measure of the pulse. Seventy beats per minute - faint and thready. Nothing to celebrate but within an acceptable range considering that the guy had just been under the knife. The bandages wrapped around his forehead no doubt concealed an impressive number of stitches. Dmitri had run Harland through the basics of the procedure, but most of it had sounded like gobbledygook.

The sequence of events that had brought him here flashed through his mind once again. If it weren't for Franklin's insistence on trying to save this man, perhaps he would already be home. He couldn't blame his friend for trying to do the right thing, but the attempt had cost both men their freedom while doing nothing to alter the fate of Colonel Mackinsky.

Harland turned over Franklin's decision in his mind and considered it afresh. Maybe sometimes the intentions of a man were more important than the results they achieved. Mackinsky had tried to use his task force to reclaim two bridges. Franklin had tried to protect the wounded colonel. Harland had tried to take on a dozen T-80s by himself.

All these attempts had been doomed from the start. And yet, there was something that could be admired about the crazy bravery of it all.

Harland glanced up and down the hallway. When he was sure no one was around, he laid a hand on the colonel's shoulder and spoke.

"Sir," he whispered. "I don't know if you can hear me or not. I'm Will Harland. Sergeant. Delta Company. 3rd Battalion. 8th Infantry Division."

Harland waited a beat and watched for any response. None came.

"Sir, I don't know if you remember me, but we used to talk whenever I had to drive you somewhere. See, I'm from Virginia, too. You used to tell me your stories about hunting and fishing when we ran into each other. I usually had no idea what you were talking about."

As he gazed upon the colonel, a renewed sense of purpose flooded through the fibers of Harland's being. It was a time for crazy acts of bravery. This was war. Men either took chances or they gave in to the misery of it all. Whatever had happened before, they were still alive and that in itself was enough reason to gamble on a better future.

He leaned over the sleeping figure of Ted Mackinsky and whispered.

"Sir, we're getting the hell out of here!"

BLIND

Sergeant Haight patted his breast pocket to confirm the presence of his precious pack of Marlboros. Sure enough, they sat there waiting for his return to basecamp where he could finally light up again. As soon as this foray into enemy territory was over, he would stick his head under a poncho and light up. Oh, how nice it would feel!

Haight could almost taste the silky inhalations followed by the rush of that old nicotine high. It was his own little island of pleasure amid an ocean of physical and mental strain. When the war started, he called off his plans to quit, convinced that he would need his usual dose of relief. Some nights – like tonight – were unmanageable without it.

The troubles had started right away. First, he had taken his squad down the eastern slope of the hill upon which Fox Troop's hidden basecamp was located. Convinced that the huge clumps of thick forest would offer great concealment for his men, they had trudged through the trees in the darkness. The vegetation was so dense that their night vision goggles were largely useless. Everything just looked like indistinguishable dark blobs. About halfway down the slope, a headcount revealed that three of his men had gone missing.

They all stood around like idiots at the rally point for ten infuriating minutes before Haight went off to look for his lost sheep.

Were they dead or captured? Had they run off without a word? As he passed through the bristling thorn bushes that pricked and poked at his skin, he debated about whether or not to abort the mission and return to camp or just go on without them. A frantic ten-minute search revealed nothing. He gave up. When he returned to the rally point to deliver the bad news, he found all three men waiting there. "Frustrating" didn't even begin to describe it.

With everyone in the squad accounted for, they moved toward the objective. The mission was to conduct an area reconnaissance far to the east of Hünfeld. They had followed Highway 7 north, only to find that crossing the road was nearly impossible. A dozen armored vehicles sat just off the shoulder. A steady stream of enemy supply trucks trundled along the road.

Haight felt a series of hard taps on his shoulder. He didn't have to wonder who it was this time. Private Thomas lay next to him in the undergrowth. The kid loomed large and green in his night vision goggles. Thomas pointed at the map and cupped his hand. After looking at the marked location, Haight understood what Thomas was proposing.

To the south, a company's worth of destroyed West German Leopards and Marders littered the ground around the highway. Because of all the dead tanks and infantry carriers, the enemy was more dispersed in that area. No doubt the Russians were waiting for an armored recovery vehicle to come along and drag all that junk away. Perhaps the vehicles would conceal the squad's approach to the highway. It was worth a shot.

When they arrived near the wrecks, Haight called a halt and ordered his men to stay behind while he scouted forward. Little had changed since they were here ten minutes ago. From behind the mangled hull of a burnt Leopard 1 tank, Haight spied two SAM vehicles interspersed among a string of charred metal hulks. They were roughly three hundred meters apart without line of sight to each other.

How simple it would be to just sneak up on the nearby SA-8 vehicles, drop a pair of grenades inside, then scoot over the highway like nothing ever happened. No one would probably notice until the next morning.

The only problem was that Fitzgerald had been crystal clear in his briefing – they were under strict orders not to engage the enemy. He clenched his teeth and grumbled to himself. Easy for him to say!

Haight mentally plotted a course through the maze of smoldering vehicles that would take them as far as the highway. The likelihood of being spotted was nearly zero. He was sure of it. When he returned to his men at the rally point, he informed them of the way forward and broke up his squad into three groups of three men each.

Haight kept his eyes on the highway as it grew closer through his night vision. When he was less than a hundred yards from the road's edge, a truck pulled off to the side of the highway and squealed to a halt. Eight figures disembarked. The American scouts hit the dirt.

An electric shock of fear pulsed through Haight's mind as the Russians trudged toward him. He flicked the safety off his M16 and considered the consequences. If they started a gun battle, they would soon find themselves surrounded by a much larger force. At first light, the enemy would find them here and it would all be over.

Haight scanned around him for a hiding place, but there was nothing. He motioned to his men to spread themselves out and go prone. The command was passed down the line to the rest of his squad and soon enough they were just nine more corpses among the dozens already there.

Haight unholstered his pistol and tucked his arm underneath his body. The hard metal dug into his stomach. He had already made up his mind. Sergeant Haight would not be captured. He would rather go out fighting than spend any time under pain-wracked hours of interrogation by some Communist S.O.B.

The Russians talked loudly as they approached. Haight squeezed his eyes shut and focused on keeping as still as possible. An itch developed on his right calf and Haight tried his best to ignore it. Each passing second, it grew increasingly unbearable. He bit down hard on his lip and tried to keep his mind away from the intense need to just reach down and scratch the area.

Unable to kill the insatiable urge, Haight brought his hand down one half-inch at a time. Somewhere to his left, a boot thudded on the soft ground. Someone shouted in Russian and Haight forgot all about the itch. He squeezed the pistol grip and waited for someone to turn him over. When they did, they were in for one hell of a surprise.

Someone laughed and Haight wondered if he had already been discovered. That had to be it. They had seen him a mile off and now they were mocking his cowardly efforts. A flash of heat filled his chest. Haight held his breath and braced himself for the shot.

It never came.

Something slid around his chest and dug into his breast pockets. A probing set of fingers danced against his chest. After an interminable ten seconds, the hand clamped around Haight's pack of cigarettes and yanked them out. His arms tensed in outrage at the act of thievery and he mentally cursed the thief. You Russian bastard!

Next came the metallic flick of a lighter followed by a soft exhalation and more chatter in Russian. Haight considered the pistol in his hands and listened to someone else smoke his prized Marlboros. The wonderful aroma of burnt tar and nicotine flowed into his nostrils and he clenched his jaw in impotent anger. Smoke up, Ivan. Someday I'll steal those back from your real corpse.

From off in the distance came an angry shout, like a father beckoning an unruly child. The lit cigarette butt landed inches from Haight's face. Its heat swept against his cheek as the filter burned down. Something nearby shattered as the Russians clomped off southwest - away from his fellow scouts. When Haight was sure they were gone, he opened his eyes a crack and took a careful look around. A glance to his right revealed his mangled night vision goggles. A cursory examination was enough to determine they would never work again.

Once over the highway, the group of scouts passed east through the fields. Occasionally, they stopped to note anything of interest.

Positions of mobile SAMs and AAA were recorded along with any sign of enemy activity. By the time they reached their destination, Haight was convinced that something big was happening.

When a transport aircraft descended through a low bank of clouds and dropped to the strip of highway below, everything fell neatly into place. After snapping dozens of photographs and filling a whole book's worth of sketches, he decided to call it a night. The journey back to camp was slow and painstaking. The first strands of sunlight loomed over the nearby hills just as they arrived home.

PUZZLIN' EVIDENCE

Colonel Evans studied the photos in front of him and wondered if they were enough to win the war. Like a lawyer in a courtroom, all he could do was show the proof and urge General Bill Taylor to act accordingly. The man was a high-ranking aide to V Corps' lieutenant general and his opinion was vital for getting the green light for operations throughout CENTAG.

If this guy could be swayed, then the future looked just a little brighter for special operations warfare and perhaps the outcome of the conflict. If not, Evans would be forced to continue running his rinky-dink ops on a shoestring and hope that the rest of NATO's generals could achieve victory without his help. Evans braced himself for probable rejection – and not without good reason.

The spectacular failure of Operation First Strike had caused the brass to shy away from taking chances. When the 8th Infantry Division's commander had been ordered to send reinforcements to assist the flailing efforts of Task Force Lance, he had balked and unilaterally aborted the operation because it hadn't gone as smoothly as predicted. The result was a military disaster so complete that it would be taught at military academies for generations to come.

The punishment for such antics was an immediate transfer to the Pentagon where the former 8ID commander would serve the rest of his career counting paperclips.

The intended message of such censure was somehow misunderstood by several key field commanders as 'Don't take any chances' when it was instead meant to convey the opposite. The idea of a counterattack in the early stages of the war was commendable. It was the lack of follow-through that was inexcusable. Evans and a few others had understood that. Others had not.

Evans pointed to the large screen in front of him and placed the first image on the overhead projector. The dark outlines of a Soviet transport aircraft were barely visible against an emerald green sky. The image had been captured with the newer infrared cameras and although they were stunning pieces of technology, it was still hard to make out distinct shapes.

The scouts of Fox Troop had bravely stayed in the danger area and snapped dozens of pictures. They had done their job admirably and now it was his turn to carry the ball further down the field. In order to sell the concept of a stay-behind military force in enemy occupied areas, he would need to apply the age-old principles taught to every Madison Avenue acolyte – A.I.D.A. Attention. Interest. Decision. Action.

Evans cleared his throat and spoke in deliberate confident tones.

"Sir, these photos were taken by assets located near Fulda," he said. "As you can see, we have several Soviet An-12 transports lined up here along Route 84 about eight klicks east of Hünfeld. You can see in the foreground the shapes of several vehicles. These are mobile surface-to-air vehicles that are interspersed throughout the area. The planes you're looking at are landing on a highway that's been converted to serve as an airstrip."

The dark smoky room was filled only with the whir of the projector's cooling fan. Davis sat stone-faced at the table with his aides on either side of him. Evans took a moment to wonder if he was wasting his time, then continued anyway.

"It seems obvious the Soviets have ripped a page right out of our own playbook. I know you were here during Exercise Highway '84 when we converted the Ahlhorn Highway Strip into a runway for our C-130s and A-10s. The Russians appear to have followed our principles to the letter, removing guardrails and lights as well as pouring concrete along the side of the road to expand its width. The scouts reported a chemical spray being applied to the pavement, and we presume that is some kind of anti-skid coating. Whatever it is, they've done an admirable job of using it to transform a large chunk of road into a makeshift airfield. Last night, they were landing planes at a rate of roughly twelve per hour."

Davis leaned over to his right and murmured to one of his cronies. The silhouettes turned toward each other and nodded vigorously. Evans placed a map of the local area on the projector and took a moment to admire the carefully drawn arrows and lines near Hünfeld.

"The airfield itself isn't as interesting as what's actually happening after the planes land. The Cubs are unloaded by ground crews and supplies are then loaded aboard columns of waiting trucks. The vehicles move west until they hit Highway 7. Half the trucks turn north and drive for Niederaula while the others go south to Fulda. It's from these two cities that the Soviet 8th Guards Army is currently driving west in a two-pronged attack aimed at capturing Frankfurt."

The quiet mutters broke out into a jumble of voices. Davis puffed on his cigar and raised a beefy finger. Evans offered him a polite smile and waited for the question.

"Colonel, I would like you to take a minute and explore the question of 'why' they're doing this. Can you detail that further?" asked Davis.

Evans knew a request for simplification when he saw it. He had to be careful. Complication would give Davis a reason not to commit. On the other hand, the last thing Evans wanted was to appear condescending.

"Sir, I think it's important to remember that the main issue that the Soviets are facing is the lack of roads available to fit all their combat and support vehicles flowing in from East Germany. As you know, the rate of fuel and ammunition consumption has been much higher than either side anticipated. The increasing demand to resupply their combat units has meant that supply trucks have taken priority over combat reinforcements. This dilemma has slowed the Soviet advance as it moves west. By bringing in supply from the air, the Soviets are getting around the problem entirely. This way, they free up the roads for their follow-on forces."

Davis leaned forward in his chair and jabbed a finger toward the screen. Evans took a shaky breath and tried to remember the next step in the process. What was it again? Ah yes. Decision.

The baritone voice of General Davis boomed through the room.

"If that's the case, this should be moved to air operations. Get a flight package together immediately and bomb the hell out of them."

"Sir, the major obstacle to an airstrike is the large amount of anti-aircraft assets in the area," said Evans. "I've already crunched the numbers with our air planners. Hitting the target, even with guided munitions, would mean losing at least a squadron's worth of strike aircraft. Considering that we've already taken heavy hits, I don't know how we can afford those kinds of losses at the moment."

A heavy silence consumed the briefing room. Evans paced back and forth as if he were considering his options. In truth, he had anticipated all this down to the last detail. Briefings were a matter of theatrics as much as they were about the facts. All he had to do was show a way out of the darkness. When it was time, he came to an abrupt halt and held up a finger.

"However - I have assets in the area on loan from 2/11 ACR," said Evans. "Perhaps we could put those to use in cutting down the amount of flak around the target."

General Davis' eyes went wide as if someone had just waved the world's juiciest twelve-ounce steak in front of a starving man.

"Do you really think that would work? I need a way to stall the Russians. We have defensive operations being prepared near Phase Line Gulfport and Fargo. Dammit! If we just had a little more TIME! Are you sure you can buy us that, colonel?"

Evans was shocked by the man's sudden release of emotion. Were things really as bad as he suspected?

"I have the utmost confidence, sir. Of course, the planning and coordination would go a lot smoother if you're willing to hand over these assets to my office. The regimental commander has requested the immediate return of Fox Troop, but I'll need those men and vehicles for at least twenty-four more hours."

Davis slammed a palm on the table with all the righteousness of the freshly converted.

"Colonel Evans, if you can pull this off, I'll personally see to it that you have those ground troops on permanent loan. Someone from air ops will get in touch with you right away. Don't you worry about that."

"Thank you, sir," said Evans.

Davis and his aides filed out of the room, leaving Evans alone. Finally, the sweat poured down from his face and his knees buckled. Unable to hold back the wave of gut-clenching nervousness, he placed both palms on the table and counted as he exhaled long hot breaths. When calm returned, he allowed himself just the smallest of grins.

In one fell swoop, he had expanded his force and secured a vital operation. No more would he go begging for a helicopter to drop off his men or an extra crate of ammunition. If this operation went smoothly, he could ask for more. The momentum was growing in his favor. If it continued this way, he might yet salvage a victory for his country.

"I already let one Mackinsky nearly get us all killed," said White. "I'm not gonna sit here and let another one do it. We're coming with you." The lieutenant slid down into the cupola and racked the .50 caliber machinegun as if he were Chuck Norris in an action movie.

"I would not advise that," Fitzgerald said. "If we go out there with tanks, we'll lose the element of surprise. They'll be on us like syrup on pancakes before we fire our first shot."

White rolled his eyes and spoke on the intercom to the driver. The tank's massive engine whirred to life.

"You don't get it," White shouted. "You'll be caught out there with your butts over the fire when those Dragon missiles are gone. Ivan's gonna come at you with tanks and you'll be goners before you can get back here. You need armor support!"

Fitzgerald put his hands on his hips and stepped back from the Abrams. Mackinsky had been clear enough in his operations details. None of White's tanks were to be anywhere near the area of operations. They were to stay put in the clearing while the scouts went out and took out a dozen anti-aircraft vehicles near the target.

"B-but there's no need," the second lieutenant insisted. "My scouts can take care of it!"

"MY scouts can take care of it," said White. "But they'll need help. You guys carry out the main operation.

When it's time to pull back, we'll be out there to cover you."

Fitzgerald had to admit it made a certain amount of sense. Once the aircraft struck with their bombs and missiles, his scouts would be most vulnerable as they pulled away from their objectives and returned home. If any Russian tanks followed, the scouts would be in big trouble.

White ran through the modified plan, pointing out the three clusters of anti-aircraft sites positioned in a triangular pattern around the town of Hünfeld. Each of Fitzgerald's squads had been assigned to take out three vehicles per site. The rest would be left for the Wild Weasel aircraft to deal with before the main attack hit the airfield proper.

When it was time to pull back, White's three Abrams would charge around the low hills to the south of the town and sweep around to the north in a giant counterclockwise fashion. Any pursuing Russian armor would be engaged and destroyed while Fitzgerald's infantry made a dash for the base camp. The more Fitzgerald thought about the new plan, the more he liked it. Maybe White knew what he was doing, after all.

Maybe.

***

Sergeant Haight kneeled in the tall weeds near the crest of Hill 212 and watched as three of his two-man Dragon teams set up just short of the tree line. The area directly behind them had been quietly cleared of grass and other flammable objects, so as to keep the weapon's backblast from igniting a fire. From here, they had a clear line of sight over the gentle rolls of pitted grassland that filled the distance between Haight's men and the makeshift airstrip.

Thanks to a liberal application of concrete, the highway had been hastily widened to accommodate aircraft. Ground crews rushed back and forth among the parked aircraft while construction vehicles built hardened shelters to the north. Surrounding the entire operation were six anti-aircraft vehicles perched atop a bulldozed layer of earth.

Haight watched another four-engine aircraft lumber down from the gloomy bank of low-hanging clouds.

Upon touching down, the plane jolted to the right before the pilot corrected its course.

The engines cut halfway before the Antonov reached a long strip of safety netting that resembled a giant red volleyball net. Once it became apparent that this was a "good" landing, the netting was quickly pulled away and the aircraft slowed of its own accord. Soon, it was directed off the highway, where it taxied to a large circular unloading area. The rear ramp descended and the waiting ground crew rushed aboard to unload its contents into four huge Ural trucks.

The blackened carcasses of two transport planes sat in the nearby field. Apparently, a couple of pilots had failed to slow their approach to compensate for a much rougher landing than usual. Despite that, the Soviet operation seemed to be going quite smoothly. Already another Russian aircraft was gently descending toward the highway. If all went well, it would be the last one. Very soon, a package of NATO aircraft would come along and turn the whole thing into a flaming mass of debris. Haight hoped the guy who had the audacity to steal his smokes was down there.

All three Dragon teams gave the ready signal. They were to hit a SAM radar vehicle and a pair of ZSU anti-aircraft guns that sat just off the runway. Both tracked vehicles bristled with four large automatic cannons that could fire thousands of rounds per minute at low-flying aircraft. Atop the weapons mount was a circular radar dish that served a vital part of the vehicle's fire control center. Since the NATO strike package would be carrying out a low-level approach, the mobile SAMs were not a high priority. Those would be handled by the Wild Weasel aircraft, which would sniff out their radar emissions and launch homing missiles at their positions.

Surrounding the air defense vehicles was a pair of T-62s. The hulking tanks sat out in the field like crocodiles basking in the sun. Haight would have liked to have taken them out along with the anti-aircraft vehicles, but he only had three launchers. He considered shooting the tanks with the first wave of missiles and then reloading and hitting the ZSUs but by then the element of surprise would be lost. As a result, the plan was simply to fire three missiles then get the Hell out of here.

Haight grabbed the portable radio handset and keyed it twice. His hand shook as he waited for the response.

Three low tones would indicate that the other two squads over to the north and west of Hünfeld were ready to fire on their targets. As he held the handset to his ear, Haight picked up the binoculars and scanned the target area once again. Three Urals bounced along the side of the road and parked near the aircraft. From the back of the trucks emerged two Russians who screamed while brandishing their weapons. Seconds later, a ragged group of men poured out from the canvas truck bed.

Haight's stomach curdled as he squinted at the column of hobbling figures. He reached over and jabbed Thomas' shoulder while offering the binoculars. The private grabbed them and held them up to his face.

"Friendlies," Taylor murmured. After a pause, he repeated the word.

Haight pressed down hard on the handset.

"Friendlies in the target area," he said. "Repeat. We have friendlies at the target. Abort. Abort the mission. Abort."

The only response was three short clicks. Haight's grip tightened as he begged and pleaded. The skies to the west came alive with the scream of jet engines. Any second now, they would be here. Over the hills to the north and west came a string of cracks as the other squads went to work with their missiles. Haight dropped the headset and spat out a dozen swear words. With his eyes closed tight, he raised his arm to give the signal. Seconds later, the anti-tanks missiles whisked toward their targets.

The commander of one of the ZSUs leapt off the vehicle and hugged the ground. The first missile slammed into the side of his vehicle and exploded in a great orange ball of flame. Metal pieces spewed upward for a dozen meters then showered down around the wreckage. Almost at the same instant, the radar truck met the same fate.

The remaining ZSU was untouched. The Dragon team that had fired at it was busy with a pair of pliers, trying to cut the wire to the missile. A look through the binoculars revealed the source of the problem. The missile's motor had cut out halfway to the target. Without any forward means of propulsion, the thing had just dropped to a knoll and now sat there inert.

With the guidance wires still attached to the launcher, the crew was attempting to cut them in an effort to reload and fire again.

Haight waved at the two-man team. Neither of them turned his way, so consumed were they with their task. Unable to get their attention, he cupped his hands around his mouth and screamed in their direction.

"Leave it! Take cover!"

The warning came too late. The ZSU's turret swiveled and let loose a torrent of anti-aircraft fire straight at the Dragon team's position. The 23mm rounds blasted into the hillside. When the shooting stopped, there was nothing left of the Dragon team. Giant clouds of dust billowed up from the ground. Haight lobbed out smoke grenades and shouted at his men to get back to base. Taylor stood up to run and Haight yanked him back down.

"No! You're with me!" he said. "I want to check something."

The plane swooped in at tree-top level. Haight closed his eyes and said a prayer for the friendlies caught in the ensuing firestorm.

***

Captain Mark "Poncho" Faircloth pushed the A-10's flightstick forward and hugged the ground as a stream of fire punched at the airframe. At this altitude, there was very little room to maneuver and trying to do so was an invitation to crash and cartwheel the big ugly plane. Instead, he rode on through each thud and bang while talking gently to his aircraft as if he were breaking in one of the bucks on his father's farm back in Montana.

"Come on, girl. You can do it. Let's get there."

A glance to Faircloth's left revealed his wingman, Greg "Batman" Mellis, was still limping along beside him. The A-10 Warthog he piloted was trailing a dark stream of smoke from his right engine. In peacetime, they would have aborted the run and returned to base immediately. These days, the unspoken rule was that unless a plane was doomed, the mission continued on regardless. Faircloth wanted to talk to Mellis, but they were radio silent. He would have to trust that his wingman was not suicidal enough to keep flying a broken airplane straight into the ground.

A series of fresh jolts brought Faircloth's attention back to his head-up display. The rectangular piece of glass in front of him showed everything a pilot needed to know at a glance. At this particular moment, he was concerned with the Time-To-Target indicator, which showed he would be over his next waypoint in less than thirty seconds. In no way did he take any sort of relief at this information. To a ground attack pilot in hostile airspace, a half-minute felt like an aeon.

Faircloth pitched the nose up just slightly to account for a sudden rise in the terrain ahead. As he gained altitude, his radar warning receiver chirped. His heart battered his ribcage as he soaked in the fact that an enemy SAMs radar had detected his aircraft and was in the process of locking him up. Just after cresting the hill, Faircloth inched the plane's nose back down. The diamond-shaped warning symbol on the front dash winked out. Relief washed over him. One of the escorting F-4 "Wild Weasel" aircraft had presumably just put an anti-radiation missile up the tailpipe of the pesky SA-8.

"See, little lady? Nothing to worry about."

With ten seconds left until it was time to release his cluster bombs, his eyes flicked down to the waypoint indicator and he brought the plane into a gentle left turn. Just over his shoulder lay the town of Hünfeld, a mere blip on the map that he would pass by in seconds. Beyond it to the east were the tell-tale signs of dark smoke that indicated the ground forces had done their job and whittled down the heavy presence of anti-aircraft guns near the target.

Another sharp rise and fall in the terrain brought the airfield in sight. He slid the throttle back and fought against the urge to lift away from the ground. Something blinked just ahead of him and then came a racket like the slams of a screen door in summer. Faircloth watched his wingman nose straight into the ground and explode. He cranked the stick hard left to line up the target.

"It's okay, girl. Almost there. We got this."

A warning light flashed on his dash and Faircloth jammed a finger hard against the Master Caution button.

A few seconds of hard right rudder brought his aircraft over the top of the converted highway strip. Just ahead of him sat a neat column of aircraft, trucks, and people. A three second belch of 30mm cannon fire sent a string of explosions racing in front of his path. The plane slowed from the massive cannon's recoil and Faircloth fought stick and rudder to keep the A-10 on course.

With his bombing reticule centered on the first big plane, he rippled his bombs off one by one. No longer burdened by the extra weight of the ordnance, his aircraft leapt upward on its own accord. Faircloth stomped on the left rudder and cranked the stick as he turned for home. His guts clenched as the high-g turn shoved him back hard into the seat. The horizon settled and Faircloth brought the throttle forward in a bid to keep the aircraft from stalling.

Behind him, the submunitions crunched like a giant hailstorm as they rained down on the highway and detonated. Hundreds of the little bombs exploded in a wave of utter destruction that tore through the enemy aircraft and vehicles over which he had flown.

Faircloth had no time to wonder if the hits were good – he was already dodging more flak as he traveled west. When he finally arrived back at Sembach Air Base, Faircloth climbed down the cockpit ladder and waited for his legs to stop shaking. His A-10 was a mess. The airframe sported a donut shop's worth of holes, and the leading edge of the right wing looked as though it had been gnawed off by some giant beast. That he had made it back to base was a minor miracle.

WILD WILD LIFE

Three M1 tanks raced along the base of Hill 395 with White's Abrams in the lead. Standing in the cupola with the engine whining and the hot wind rushing toward his face was like a slice of Heaven for a tanker. Cooped up at the base camp, he had nearly forgotten how great it was to be riding through the countryside, wrapped in thick Chobham armor and impervious to almost everything out there. With a bit of luck, Torrence had even managed to fix the tank's primary sight. Everything was set to rock and roll.

White licked his lips as he thought of the scouts, who were no doubt sprinting to get away from the confusion and death that surrounded the highway airstrip. Although he hadn't seen the bombs hit, he definitely heard the explosions and smelled the aftermath. His nostrils burned every time he took a breath, but it felt good and it reminded him that his men had played a key role in delivering death and destruction to the enemy. Surely, there would be something left for him too. He rubbed his gloved hands together in anticipation.

"Target! Three o'clock!" shouted Torrence. White ducked down inside the tank, where the temperature was warmer by ten degrees. Torrence peered through the sight as he leaned over in his seat. White held down the PTT button and spoke over the intercom.

"What do you have for me?"

"T-62. Range…580."

White gave him the all-clear and the main gun blasted out a round at the Soviet vehicle. The loader turned and grabbed another round from the ready rack. Both M1s on either side of his tank fired in rapid one-two succession. White looked through the vision blocks near his hatch and caught sight of three burning T-62s.

Off to his left, the scouts were running up along the hill's steep slope, dashing from cover to cover as they fled from the pursuing Russians. White gave a thumbs up in their direction and told his driver, Private Sanchez, to pick up the pace. The tank bounded up the hillocks and ran down the depressions as if it were a boat riding the waves of a frozen ocean. White felt his gut drop as they charged up another incline, only to spot a milky contrail to his right.

"Missile!" he shouted. "Incoming missile. Drive!"

Sanchez gunned the engine and brought the Abrams into the next miniature valley. It was just big enough to fit his tank. The other tanks beside him continued straight ahead toward cover. White motioned to each of the commanders to indicate the distant threat. Seconds later, the ear-splitting crash and grind of metal poured out from somewhere to his right. White called out over the radio but received no response from Two Two. Twin tentacles of dark smoke drifted upward from its position.

White directed his Abrams forward to a hull down firing position. With only the turret of the Abrams visible to the enemy, he had a much better chance of surviving any incoming fire. Torrence announced the presence of two T-62s sitting side-by-side just to the southeast of Hünfeld. Both tanks were dug-in. A look through the binoculars confirmed the sighting. Only the top parts of the turrets were barely visible with 4x magnification at nearly 500 meters.

"Hit it!" said White. "Take out the left one."

Torrence checked the auxiliary sight to confirm the lay of the main gun. Meanwhile, the Abrams to his left fired off a round that slammed home, striking the T-62's front turret and dissecting the squat round hunk of metal from the hull. White watched as the main gun of the remaining tank sparked up like a plastic lighter. In the intervening distance, he caught sight of the flame and smoke of another guided missile reaching out towards his position.

Although his brain screamed at him to reverse the tank, White directed Torrence to target the remaining T-62 with their only remaining SABOT round. It cost precious seconds to line up the enemy tank and fire. The enemy tank erupted in a dirty orange ball of flame but White kept his eyes glued to the incoming missile.

With no one left alive to guide it, the AT-8 shot meters over White's head and plowed into Hill 395 two hundred meters to his rear. The entire crew scanned for further targets to their front and sides but found none. White ordered the Abrams up over the hillock where he found the occupants of tank Two Two wandering around in a daze outside of the vehicle. The right side of the turret was a dark bulge of smoking steel. The impact panels on the turret deck had blown.

White called the commander over and gestured toward the wounded beast.

"Bad luck!" shouted White. In truth, he was relieved to see that none of the men were dead. Although the missile had severely damaged the tank, the automatic fire suppression system had already doused most of the flames. The tank's loader was badly burned on his arms and chest. Both the driver and the gunner sat him on the ground and pulled out a roll of gauze. White couldn't bare to look at the wounded man. It had been his idea to come out here and play cowboy and someone else had paid the price for it.

When the man was bandaged up, the commander of Two Two dumped a WP grenade down the tank's hatch. All four crewmembers climbed aboard White's tank and grabbed hold of the bustles.

As White's tanks continued its maneuver around the base of the hill, he whistled at the utter devastation wrought upon the highway by the A-10s. Everything along Route 84 was aflame. Transport aircraft and supply trucks burned and exploded as men ran back and forth in a futile effort to douse the inferno. There were no targets to call out.

Delay-fuse bomblets cooked off here and there, incinerating the rescue teams that were busy hauling the unfortunate survivors out of mangled airframes. White felt none of the exhilaration he expected at the sight of such misery. Instead, his heart was filled with pity.

Before signing up for the army, White had spent two years working as a prison guard at a maximum-security facility back home in West Texas. The prison had been filled with the scum of the earth. He would not have wished this fate on any one of those men.

"Dear God in Heaven," he muttered. White said a silent prayer for the victims of the tragedy and turned the tanks back toward the base camp.

***

Lieutenant Fitzgerald counted the men as they returned and jotted each name down on his yellow notepad. Despite the mission's inherent dangers and the last-minute change of plan, casualties had been surprisingly light. Two men had died after taking fire from an anti-aircraft vehicle. Two more were seriously wounded when Sergeant Hellman's squad had stumbled into a minefield on the way back from their ambush site.

It was a favorable exchange rate considering that the Russians had just lost countless supply trucks and a squadron of transport aircraft. Of course, someone would need to get out there and do a proper bomb damage assessment and crunch the actual numbers – but Fitzgerald was convinced they would hold up his early conclusions. He looked back over his list and noted the physical condition of each man. As he went down the names, he noticed that two were missing.

Fitzgerald walked over to a tangle of combat netting and ducked his head underneath. A half-dozen scouts sat cross-legged in the shade. Painted camouflage faces glared back at Fitzgerald, no doubt wondering at his demands. Fitzgerald tried his best to smile. It felt awkward and forced.

"Corporal Foote, if you have a moment," he said.

The gangly nineteen-year-old followed Fitzgerald toward the edge of the clearing. When he was sure he was out of earshot of the other men, Fitzgerald asked him about Haight and Taylor. Foote was a competent scout and was known as a straight shooter among the officers.

Unfortunately, the young man had developed a bad stutter since the first time Fox Troop had seen combat. Fitzgerald wondered if it was a new habit or if stress had unleashed an old speech disorder that had been quelled long ago.

"Th-they t-took off right a-after," said Foote. "N-north."

Fitzgerald put a hand up. "Got it," he said. The young man retreated to the comfort of the netting, leaving only more questions in his wake. Why hadn't Haight and Taylor come back with the rest of their squad? If they were captured, it wouldn't be long before they would reveal the location of the base camp. As soon as White returned from his little joyride, they would need to drop everything and move away from here. It was the only way.

He marched to the center of the clearing and whistled to get the attention of the scouts. Soon, he had three ranks of men standing at attention in front of him. A count confirmed that two men were absent. Fitzgerald shot a nervous glance to the sky and wondered if their coordinates weren't being fed into some artillery gunner's ballistic computer right now.

"Has anyone here seen or heard from Sergeant Haight or Private Taylor?" he boomed.

Only the hush of wind rustling through the trees came in response. Fitzgerald sighed and checked his watch. They needed to go right now. Where the hell was White?

"I want everyone ready to move out in two minutes," said Fitzgerald. "Get your stuff and form up back here. If you can't carry it with you then leave it behind. I want the radio antenna disassembled and ready to go. Move!"

As the men broke ranks and scrambled for their gear, Fitzgerald threw his books into his pack and tossed in a couple of magazines for his M16. After a minute, half of his men were back in ranks and ready to move out. Before he could give the order, someone shouted near the edge of the clearing.

Fitzgerald marched over to find Haight and Taylor doubled over and breathing as if they had just completed a marathon. He took the offered sketch book from Taylor's hands and flipped through it. One of the pencil drawings looked like a stadium bordered by barb fence and guard towers.

On the field and in the stands were figures in fatigues. The next page showed a detailed map of the outside of the stadium.

"What am I looking at?" asked Fitzgerald.

Haight gulped in a breath of air and muttered. "Hünfeld. Prison camp."

Fitzgerald leaned closer and examined the drawings. A POW camp?! How had they missed it? They had been operating in this area long enough to find it a hundred times. A look at the map revealed the probable cause. The stadium was in a large wooded sports park. From afar, it would have blended in with the natural scenery – hidden in plain sight.

"I've included every bit of information we could get about it," said Haight. "Troop strength, hardware, and estimated numbers of prisoners."

Lost in thought, Fitzgerald didn't even hear White's tanks return from their foray into enemy territory. He only noticed the lieutenant had returned when he barged toward Fitzgerald, demanding to know why all his men were lined up like tin soldiers and ready to move out.

White's demeanor shifted as Fitzgerald showed him the sketches and Haight spat out the report once again. A devilish grin spread across White's face and he dismissed both scouts.

"You know what I'm thinking?" asked White.

"No. Negative. No way," said Fitzgerald.

"C'mon! We can't just leave 'em there," said White.

"Because for one, we don't have the firepower. Even with your tanks and a platoon of infantry, we're still looking at some pretty hefty defenses in the area. Second - even if we do rescue the prisoners, where do we fit them? The reports here are at over one hundred men. We could let some ride on top of our Bradleys. Maybe a few more on the tanks. Where do the others go?"

White trudged around in wide circles, trampling the soft grass down as he cursed and swore and muttered to himself. Fitzgerald said nothing the whole time, half-worried that the man would have some sort of breakdown and just give up.

The big Texan stopped suddenly in his tracks and pivoted toward Fitzgerald.

"You missed one thing, buddy," he said. "We can reach out and touch someone now. We tell Mackinsky about the camp. Get some helos over here for support. Then move in together. When it's all done, we just chopper on out as a great big team."

Fitzgerald let the numbers roll around in his head. If the right support were provided and if the Russians didn't come charging back here in ten minutes with a division of angry guys, there was certainly a chance it could work. Great big IF. Fitzgerald wiped a palm across his face and wondered what he was getting himself into.

"Alright," said Fitzgerald. "I'll talk to Mackinsky."

Peter Mackinsky tried not to hope as he scanned the black and white photographs splayed out on the table in front of him. He plucked one out of the group and studied it. The three other men in his team took the cue and grabbed at the pile of pictures.

He could clearly discern the bird's-eye-view of an oval-shaped soccer stadium that had been turned into a prison camp. The long shadows cast by the day's last light obscured much of the details, but it was plain to see the boxy guard towers and the fencing that surrounded it. His attention was drawn like a magnet to the tiny figures in the stands and on the grounds. Somewhere among them was his father. He just knew it!

Colonel Evans stood on the opposite side of the table and gestured toward the photos.

"Those came in less than an hour ago." he said. "Courtesy of the 26th Tactical Reconnaissance Wing."

"How many prisoners?" asked Manny.

"We don't have an exact count," answered Evans. "Scouts have put the current numbers at somewhere around one hundred and fifty men. They're guarded by machinegun towers and armored vehicles. The guards appear to have been drawn from the rear security elements of the 79th Guards Tank Division."

"Wait a second. All this for a hundred and fifty guys?!" said Bates. "I thought we were gonna hit a major prison camp!"

Evans drew in a breath and sat down. He looked directly at Peter as he spoke in the kind of subdued tones usually reserved for funerals.

"This isn't a prison camp," said Evans. "It's a node in the Soviet detainment system."

Mackinsky had never heard the term before.

"A node. I don't follow, sir," he said.

"It's like a weigh station," said Evans. "Prisoners are brought there and sorted out before being sent on to larger camps further east. We suspect there are dozens of these nodes located not far behind enemy lines. This is the first one we've managed to pinpoint. With any luck, we'll be able to find out more details about the others from this raid. We'll also have liberated valuable personnel who can return to their units and resume the fight. As you know, things aren't going well for us. We need all the help we can get."

Mackinsky sensed a deflection and decided not to pursue this line of questioning. Evans interlaced his fingers and leaned forward. The body language was clear. Do not press further.

"What kind of assets are we looking at?" asked Manny.

"We've got helos from Task Force 158," said Evans. "Three Chinooks. Eight Blackhawks. A Kiowa."

Mackinsky looked over the chalk assignments. The Kiowa would hang back during the operation while the prisoners loaded up on the Chinooks. The Blackhawks were there to pick up Fox Troop and bring them back home after the operation ended.

"You'll have some extra help out there," said the colonel. "The cav unit. They'll be joining in the rescue with you. Unofficially, of course. The tanks will go in early and hit whatever's inside the town. The scouts will help with operations at the camp. We've coordinated times and locations already."

Tanner chuckled as he leafed through the sheet. "Those guys just helped nuke an airstrip near there. The Russians are probably stirred up like a hornet's nest. They'll be pushing tanks and men in there as soon as possible to hunt down White and his men. It's never going to work."

Evans spoke quietly. "We have a brief window of time if we move fast.

The intercepts we've picked up indicate an Operational Maneuver Group will be diverted off Route 4 near Bad Hersfeld. We can delay their movement into the area, but we need to move fast. The CIA has a major on the inside. Unfortunately, we'll have to burn the agent to pull this off. So we only get one chance."

The colonel passed out several sheets marked with timetables, map coordinates, and radio callsigns. Everything was there. All Mackinsky and his men had to do was to go in with the helicopters, cut into the fencing, and get the prisoners out of the camp.

"So this business with the cavalry is over?" asked Tanner.

"They're coming home with you. Once the operations at the camp are complete, they'll be ditching their tanks and APCs and boarding the helicopters," said Evans.

A double agent. A cavalry troop. A four man team.

The whole operation was a house built on the shakiest of foundations. Only prayers and rubber bands were there to keep it all from falling apart.

Mackinsky turned his gaze toward Manny. The big man's sour expression said it all. They were being thrown into a situation like dice on a Vegas craps table. The briefing was so thin that it was practically transparent.

Bates folded his arms and flung out his usual volley of complaints disguised as questions.

"The cav unit. Do they even have the ammo for this?"

Evans checked his watch before he tossed out the answer. "We have a resupply chopper going there right now. In about twenty minutes, they'll be dropping off a bladder of JP-8 fuel and a few boxes of ammunition. It won't be much."

After running through the operation timetable in greater detail, the team was dismissed to conduct rehearsals for an hour in the darkness outside the airbase. Mackinsky lingered in the briefing room after everyone else had left. Evans stood there with his arms folded.

"Sir, about this mission," said Mackinsky. "Is there any indication-."

"None whatsoever," said Evans. "I want you focused on your team and the rescue of all NATO detainees.

Your father is still classified as missing. He has not been confirmed as a prisoner and no sightings of him have been reported."

The clipped manner of speech was enough to convince Mackinsky to abandon the topic. Colonel Evans had a way of ending conversations by erecting a wall of passive speech that was characteristic of an official document. Mackinsky lowered his head and berated himself for even asking. He turned to leave. A hand caught his shoulder.

"Son, I really don't know if your father is down there," said Evans. His tone softened and his weathered face carried a sympathetic smile. "Hell, I hope he is. He's my friend. But I can't afford to go on that assumption. And neither can you. I had my doubts about giving this assignment to you, Peter. Don't make me regret it."

"Thank you, sir," he said. "I won't forget that. And you won't regret this."

Evans rubbed his tired eyes and dismissed Mackinsky with two words.

"I know."

WARNING SIGN

Harland trudged through the hospital, hoping to find someone – anyone who might tell him where Mackinsky had gone. He
had looked for Dmitri in the usual places, but the old doctor was
nowhere to be found. His search of the first and second floors had
yielded nothing but looks of confusion or disdain from the exhaust-
ed orderlies and medical staff. The only place left was the ground
floor. When he reached the bottom of the stairway, he grabbed the
nearest nurse and shouted at her.

"Mackinsky. Colonel Mackinsky," he said. "He can't leave here.
I'm his medical assistant."

From the scowl on the big woman's face, she clearly had no idea
what any of this meant nor had any time for it. Harland heaved a
dejected sigh as she walked off down the hall. Each clack of her heel
against the tiled floor echoed back toward him with contempt. Harland saluted her diminishing presence with a fully extended middle
finger, then turned to the front doors of the hospital and eyed the
heaps of fresh bodies that lay there in the sun.

Soon, the daily disposal truck would be here to cart off the
dead, then another truck would bring wounded soldiers here.
There seemed no end to the constant flow of suffering and death.
For every casualty who survived the horrors of this place, a dozen
perished in any number of gruesome ways.

Harland dragged his feet down the corridor and out the main entrance. The guards in front of the hospital glared at him as he examined the piles of corpses, all the while hoping that he would not find Colonel Mackinsky among them. Most of them were men in their early twenties. A few of them didn't have faces at all, but their bodies – or what was left of them – were lean and characteristic of young males. None of them sported the stocky frame of Colonel Mackinsky.

Harland wandered back up to the third floor. As he climbed the stairs, his head swarmed with questions. Had Mackinsky been sent east for interrogation already? The man had been steadily recovering since the surgery. Once or twice, he had opened his eyes for brief periods before slipping back into unconsciousness.

Harland had noticed the man's heartbeat growing stronger and his blood pressure returning to normal. In a bid to delay the inevitable, he had falsified the man's reports to make his condition seem much worse. Harland was sure Dmitri would see through the ruse, but he hadn't counted on it happening so soon.

When Harland got to the top of the stairs, he pushed open the door to find Dmitri standing in front of him with his arms folded against his chest. A wry smile worked its way across his face, as if he had known all along of Harland's futile efforts.

"You!" shouted Harland. "Where is Colonel Mackinsky? Tell me right now or so help me, I'll tear this place apart."

Dmitri said nothing but wagged a finger to beckon him further down the hall. As they walked together, he turned and delivered the grim news.

"He is stable enough to be moved east. The helicopter is here."

"Where's he headed?" demanded Harland. "Tell me."

"Leipzig."

"When?"

"Very soon," said Dmitri.

"I'm begging you," said Harland. "Help me. Keep him here until he's well enough to escape."

Dmitri shook his head. "You ask too much! I've helped you more than I should have already."

"Then get me on that flight," said Harland. He couldn't believe what he had just said. The words had shot out of his mouth without even the barest of forethought. At first, he regretted every syllable. Even if Dmitri said yes, the only thing that awaited him over there was certain death.

It seemed unlikely that the Soviets would expend the fuel and effort just to fly back a captured American sergeant. There was nothing Harland knew that the Soviets didn't already. They wouldn't even bother to interrogate him. He was as good as dead.

"You're crazy," said Dmitri. "Stay here with me. I know you lied on the reports, but I understand your reasons. You're learning quickly enough to be a valuable asset. Will. Please. Save yourself. Stay!"

The rational part of Harland screamed at him to say yes, but the time had finally come when he had to choose between self-interest and loyalty. The choices that had brought him here had led inexorably back to the question of what was worth living and dying for. Although he had hardly known Colonel Mackinsky, the man was still a fellow American soldier. The thought of letting him fly alone to his demise seemed traitorous at best, morally repugnant at worst. The void loomed in front of Harland. For the first time in his life, he stepped toward it. There were some things more important than self-preservation.

"Look," said Harland. He bit down on each word as it left his mouth. "That man is the only friend I have left in this world. Where he goes, I go. I'd rather run at the fence than stay here."

Dmitri tossed a Styrofoam cup of coffee at the overflowing trash can on the opposite side of the hall.

"Fine," he said. "It's your life."

Both men returned to the staircase and marched up the final flight of stairs together. When they walked through the door, Harland found himself on the roof of the hospital. A huge military transport helicopter sat there. In front of it was Colonel Mackinsky, lying on the stretcher with intravenous tubes sticking out of him. A peal of sympathy rang through Harland's mind as he watched the man lying there.

The helicopter's side door slid open and a slender man in a pressed olive drab uniform stepped out.

It was the first time that Harland had seen one with blue patches on the shoulders and above the cap's visor. The colors probably marked him as belonging to the KGB or GRU or any of the other million agencies that the Soviets used to carry out their dirty deeds around the globe. One thing was for certain - the guy was definitely not regular army. Harland looked over at Dmitri. For the first time ever, the Russian doctor looked scared.

Harland felt like an idiot as the conversation between the two Russians progressed. Dmitri smiled through most of it while the other man did not. After several gestures towards the helicopter and Harland, the man in the uniform turned to him and spoke in English that was slathered with a thick accent.

"The doctor says you wish to accompany your countryman," he said. "Is that true?"

Harland locked eyes with the man, whom he had already decided to call Boris.

"Yeah, that's right."

"How do I know you won't kill the man during the flight?" asked Boris.

Harland shrugged. "I had a million chances already. Dmitri left me alone with him plenty of times."

Boris' mouth tightened and he turned to the doctor again. This time, the tones were pointed and angry. Dmitri turned his face to the ground and nodded throughout most of it.

"You will come with us," spat Boris. "He has assured me that you are a competent medic. You will care for this man until we reach our destination. If you do anything that jeopardizes the health of your American friend, I assure you that you will pay very dearly for it. Am I clear?"

Harland gulped as he listened to the threat spill out as casual as a fast food order. The way he spoke was cold and matter-of-fact, which made the words all the more terrifying.

Harland glanced at Mackinsky and nodded.

"I understand."

Dmitri and Harland pushed the stretcher toward the waiting helicopter as the long blades made lazy circles in the space just above their heads.

Halfway to the rear doors, Boris pointed to the night sky and screamed.

Dmitri halted and turned his gaze to the west. The air pulsed with the sound of an entire armada of choppers coming toward them. Boris yanked a pistol from his belt.

"What is it?" asked Harland. "What's going on?"

Dmitri stared at him in a mix of horror and bewilderment.

"Helicopters," spat Boris. "American helicopters. You! How did you-!"

Boris jammed his pistol in Harland's face.

"Get him on the helicopter right now or I shoot all three of you! NOW!" he boomed.

Dmitri pulled at the head of the stretcher while Harland pushed. The whole while, Boris berated them for being too slow. The first snap of gunfire came while they were moving Mackinsky to the passenger compartment's litter. From somewhere below was the boom of an M1's main gun. Harland would have known that sound anywhere. It could only mean on thing – a rescue party had come for them! His heart soared.

If he could just stall long enough for help to arrive here, there was a decent chance for survival. Here it was – all happening right now! Harland fumbled with the IVs, getting one caught on the edge of the stretcher.

Boris, at the end of his patience, marched over and yanked the tubes out. The catheters ripped from of Mackinsky's arms and legs and dextrose solution spilled out everywhere. Before Harland could protest at what was happening, he felt the cold metal of Boris' gun pressed to his temple. The game was over.

Dmitri threw in a burlap bag marked with a red cross sewn on the front. Harland slung it over his shoulder and sat on the trembling floor of the cargo compartment. With a jolt, the helicopter lifted off. They were on their way to Leipzig.

HOUSES IN MOTION

The Blackhawks glided through the humid night air. A fork of lightning sliced through the dark sky to the east. The waves of adrenaline sent tremors up and down Peter Mackinsky's body. No one said anything as they closed in toward the objective – there was no need. Each man in the team was focused like a laser on the task laid out for them.

Mackinsky recalled the still images of the soccer stadium. Home to the Hunfelder SV club, the Rhönkampfbahn was a pitch built in the middle of a large park in the east of Hünfeld. To its north and south were two wide streets and to the east of it was a small lake. The natural area had been well-maintained by the city and used extensively by its citizens for amateur soccer games, equestrian riding, and hiking.

The open spaces made it perfect for dropping a helicopter or twelve in the middle of. The only question was whether or not White and his men were down there suppressing what remained of the anti-air defenses.

Apparently, several of the remaining ZSUs and SAM vehicles near the destroyed airfield had pulled back to Hünfeld after the air-strikes. The area around the town had been cleared of most combat units and Evans had surmised that the Soviets believed a NATO offensive was about to take place in the area.

This was no surprise, given that Lieutenant White had been operating with his tanks out there, despite orders to the contrary. In any case, the fear and confusion he had instilled upon the local Soviet commander had worked in their favor. They would have a small window of opportunity to carry out this mission and then leave.

According to the plan, the cavalry team was slated to come in from the south and kill anything and everything that looked hostile. The tanks would get there first with the APCs trailing close behind. By that time, the helicopters would land in the spacious parking lot just outside the prison camp and breach the fence.

White's scouts would surround the pitch and use their M203s to pour fire in at the guard towers. It was too bad that their 25mm chain guns were dry. The prisoners would fly out with the Chinooks. White and his men would destroy their own vehicles and board the Blackhawks. It sounded simple, but as always, there were a million hidden things that could go wrong. The biggest issue was that of timing.

If White arrived late, the Blackhawks would face heavy anti-aircraft fire coming in on the objective. If the Blackhawk pilots were tardy, the prisoners might get moved or the guards could just decide to mow them down at the first sight of American tanks.

Coordination was the key to achieving surprise. With neither team leader able to speak to the other to plan out the details of the operation, they were operating as an army of two separate entities. The danger of a screw-up was real and it weighed heavily on Mackinsky's mind as they flew low around the hills of occupied West Germany.

"Two minutes!" shouted the pilot.

Mackinsky took a deep breath. His sweat-soaked hand tightened around the rifle's grip. The thoughts of his father circled around and around in his mind like a hawk searching for prey. Each time he pushed them away, they returned.

The prospect of finding his father down there was terrifying. Equally so was the possibility that the elder Mackinsky was not down there. A cold heavy feeling sunk through his chest as the helicopters charged onward through the night sky.

On the ground below, artillery rounds crashed upon the ground and exploded like fiery blossoms that winked in and out of existence.

Occasionally, they passed over a town consumed entirely by orange and red flames. The horizon burned all around, marking the silhouettes of hills and valleys and mountains in the distance. Mackinsky didn't need to put on his night vision goggles to understand the vast scale of destruction all around him. A sniff of the heavy smoke-laden air was all one needed to understand that the entire world was burning, set ablaze by old men who refused to admit the failures of their own ideology.

Down there in the darkness was the Soviet army charging westward, relentless in its determination. Everything in front of it was going to die, and for the first time Mackinsky wondered if the war could be won. After dozens of missions behind enemy lines, it seemed that nothing he did made any real difference. Tens of thousands of sons and fathers were dying every day down there with consequences that would thunder down for generations. The scale of human tragedy was both immeasurable and unprecedented. Mackinsky decided that he had no special right to his father. The pilot shouted the one-minute warning, and Peter let go. The face of his father faded away, replaced by the steel reality of what lay ahead.

"Get ready!" Mackinsky roared.

The other men in the team pulled on their NVGs and slapped fresh magazines in their rifles.

From the ground up ahead, long hot streaks of anti-aircraft fire lashed out at them. Something slapped the fuselage and the helicopter bucked like a wild horse. Mackinsky's hand shot out to steady himself on the bulkhead. Someone screeched in the darkness.

Mackinsky held on tight to the edge of his seat and looked outside to see the Blackhawk beside them burst into flame. There was no wreckage – one minute, it was flying alongside them and now it was just gone. Only empty dead air filled the space where it flew alongside them.

"Chalk Two's gone!" he shouted.

The helicopter dipped and Mackinsky's head struck the roof, sending a sliver of pain along his spine. A sick whine clawed at his ears as tendrils of smoke seeped into the cabin like a murderer through a window.

The pilot yelped. A glance toward the cockpit revealed the co-pilot slumped over the controls. In front of him were a dozen jagged holes punched into the windshield.

"Help me!" the pilot shrieked.

Mackinsky lunged for the cockpit, wedging himself between the crew's seats. The world in front of the windshield was a tilted dark blur.

"Pull him off! I can't hold it much longer!" the pilot yelled.

Mackinsky reached for the co-pilot's arm and tugged, but the man's sleeve was stuck on the edge of the pitch lever. The ground was coming up fast with no time to carefully disentangle it. Instead, Mackinsky pulled a knife from near his combat boot and dug it into the ragged fabric of the co-pilot's flight suit. Once the pointed edge created a hole, he tore until the sleeve came loose.

Something behind him rattled like a can of spray paint. There was no time to find out what had happened. The needles in the cockpit spun counterclockwise and a crooked church steeple loomed large in the Blackhawk's path.

Mackinsky grabbed both co-pilot's shoulders and yanked him back hard into the seat. The helicopter leapt upward and tilted hard left as the Blackhawk narrowly missed colliding with the church. Mackinsky held the co-pilot back in his damaged seat. Tanner offered up a strap from his rifle and Mackinsky wrapped it around the dead man's shoulders and around the seat. The co-pilot's head lolled forward but his body remained safely away from the controls.

As the helo flared, a steady knock of small arms fire hammered into its body. The crew chief, who had been firing the occasional burst from the M134 minigun, now poured a river of hot whirling death from the Blackhawk's open passenger door.

As they descended toward the parking lot, Mackinsky grabbed his rifle and scanned the crew compartment. The smoke made it almost impossible to see.

When he switched on the night vision goggles, the batteries whined to life and the world flickered in a haze of blurry green.

On the floor of the compartment lay a huge clump that resembled a rucksack. Slowly, it took form and Mackinsky realized it was a body. Tanner leaned in close and shouted over the roar of the blades.

"Pete," he shouted. "Manny's dead."

UNISON

White was late. It wasn't his fault. The chopper that was supposed to deliver the fuel had been delayed. When it finally came, the crew helpfully dropped the bladder off five kilometers south of where they should have gone. The extra distance cost an hour's worth of marching through the steep hills to find and retrieve it.

Now they were finally riding into battle. The vehicles of White's troop drove through occupied territory as if they belonged there. They took no cover and skirted along Highway 7 the entire way. White loudly proclaimed that the area had been liberated from Soviet occupation. Everyone in his tank crew whooped and hollered even though they knew it was temporary.

When the little celebration was over, White turned a nervous glance to the map splayed out on his knees. When they were about even with Hünfeld, the entire troop wheeled right in a tight turn and sped toward the city in a diamond formation. White's two tanks rode in the lead while the Bradleys followed a hundred meters behind.

"You got anything?" asked White.

"Just ghosts," said Torrence. "Lots of wrecks."

It was just as the advance scouts had reported. The tattered remnants of a rear security company had been pulled back into Hünfeld while the rest of the Russians had pulled out in anticipation of a local counterattack.

The nearby airstrike had apparently spooked them real bad. Soon, however, they would probably be here again with more tanks than he could shake a stick at.

"I got something, sir," announced Torrence. "Pair of BMPs on the outskirts of the town. Distance nine hundred meters."

"What are they doing?" asked White.

"Just…sitting there, sir."

White peered through the sight extension to see a pair of green blobs in the distance. At higher magnification, their shape and size were obvious. Set against the cool backdrop of the stone building behind them, there was no way they could be anything but Soviet fighting vehicles.

"Let 'er rip. Engage the nearest BMP. Fire at will."

Moments later, the main gun blared and the turret quaked with the recoil. For a brief moment, it was like being inside a ringing church bell. He was ecstatic to be alive right now. No feeling would ever match that of being inside an Abrams as it hurled an anti-tank round at the enemy.

A flash in the night signaled the death of the Soviet armored vehicle. Fifty meters to White's right, Druelinger's crew fired their gun and the round slammed into the second BMP. The target flashed white and red and the flames danced in the distance like the flicker of a candle.

The M1's engine whined as it pressed on north straight up the road toward Hünfeld. White couldn't help smiling as they whizzed past the burning infantry carriers two minutes later.

Up the block near a video rental shop, he caught his first glimpse of the mobile anti-aircraft gun as its multi-barreled gun let loose a long stream of tracer fire into the night sky. From up above, he could already hear the helicopters. It was time to move fast.

"Gunner! Target that Zoo. Kill it!"

The gun pounded out another shot. This time, the blast was less than a hundred meters away. Standing in the cupola, White felt the heat ripple off the destroyed vehicle. Sparks zipped up from the hull and almost too late, he realized the vehicle's 23mm ammunition was cooking off. One of the rounds zinged off the turret side, missing him by mere inches.

White radioed Fitzgerald, who was riding in a Bradley to the rear of the tanks. It was time to let them go while the two Abrams conducted a search and destroy mission through the streets of Hünfeld.

"Cain, this is Able. Time to split." he said.

A few seconds later, Fitzgerald replied as the Bradleys turned toward the stadium.

"Good hunting, Able. Cain out."

CROSSEYED AND PAINLESS

Mackinsky watched with awe as the nearby Bradley fired off the last of its chain gun ammunition at the guard tower. The structure burst apart like a ripe tomato caught in a steel vise. All that remained was a flaming wooden pile of debris that toppled over onto the field. Thick plumes of smoke wafted through the cool night air.

The prisoners swarmed forward toward the breach. Mackinsky urged each man forward through the hole. Despite trying not to, he studied each new face that popped through on the other side of the wire.

One of the guards in another tower opened fire on the neat line of prisoners. All Hell broke loose. The column of waiting men collapsed into frantic disorder as they were cut to pieces. Groups of prisoners stampeded toward the fence, and Mackinsky winced as the front row was crushed up against the concertina wire. The ensuing howls were like something out of a nightmare.

"Get some fire on that guard tower!" he boomed.

A pair of White's scouts ran off and lobbed 40mm rounds at the platform. The first shot went wide and exploded beyond the main gate. The second smacked into the slanted roof of the tower. The chatter of the machinegun halted for a few merciful moments. Then the shots echoed out again.

Mackinsky pointed to Tanner and Bates, who were busy freeing the crushed prisoners.

It was clear they were fighting a losing battle. The captives were hopelessly entangled in the razors along the fence. Getting them out would take more time than they could afford. They would need to create more avenues of escape for the fleeing prisoners. As much as Mackinsky hated to admit it, the men caught up on the fence were a distraction.

"Make some new holes!" screamed Mackinsky.

Bates tugged at Tanner and motioned along the fence with the pair of wire cutters. Soon enough, they were working away to make a second breach. Mackinsky stepped in through the hole and waved over at the nearest group of prisoners. Soon, they were lined up again and lunging through both breaches. White's scouts led them away from the camp toward the waiting helicopters.

Mackinsky forced his gaze to meet the sight of a dozen or so bodies that littered the stadium grounds. Was his father among them? His vision blurred as his eyes grew moist.

Nearly half the prisoners were out of the camp and being loaded onto the Chinooks. White's scouts had managed to suppress one machinegun, but another one on the far side of the stadium opened up. It was like a deadly game of whack-a-mole. Mackinsky sighed and radioed for the Cobras to come, but was met instead by the sight of a light helicopter. As it swooped toward the field, it was clear that this was no gunship – it was a Kiowa.

He recognized the stylized paint job – white stripes laid over a dull green. On the bottom of the craft was a round yellow smiley face that grinned stupidly at everyone on the ground as it shot by. It was Captain Richard Lloyd. They had worked together on a few missions and the man had deservedly earned a reputation for being either astonishingly reckless or breathtakingly courageous. Most people leaned towards the former.

Mackinsky was trying frantically to wave Lloyd off as the helicopter flew a tight circle around the guard tower then came to a hover. He put his hands on his head as he realized what was happening. Lloyd was using his machine as a shield between the prisoners and the enemy gunner.

Mackinsky screamed over the radio. "Are you out of your damn mind?! Get out of there!"

Sparks danced off the frame and rotor as the pilot leaned out with an assault rifle and squeezed out a long burst at the Russian guard. The knockknockknock of the PK halted momentarily. Mackinsky watched through the green haze of the night vision goggles as Lloyd fired again.

A brief flash and a drizzle of smoke announced the demise of the machinegunner in the guard tower. The Kiowa raced back over Mackinsky's head. Somewhere just outside the makeshift prison camp came the mutter of engines. As if on cue, an M1 Abrams drove straight through the main gate. Its turret impaled the metal fencing and shoved it along for a good twenty yards before the gun swung left and pounded out a round at the remaining tower. The whole thing blew into splinters.

Mackinsky watched the tank kept continue straight through the fence. The posts that held the concertina wire popped out of the ground and a chunk of the inner wall simply gave way. The Abrams trampled over it like it wasn't even there.

The dribble of machinegun fire halted. Mackinsky realized that the Soviet guards had probably just abandoned the place – at least for now. Some officer had no doubt hopped on the radio set and called for reinforcements at the earliest sign of trouble. How much longer did they have to get out of here? Ten minutes seemed generous

TWO NOTE SWIVEL

High winds buffeted the Mi-8 Hip as it took off from the roof of the hospital. Harland sat near the back of the darkened crew compartment, clutching the medical bag that Dmitri had packed for him. Mackinsky lay on the nearby litter. Dark streaks of blood oozed from where Boris had ripped out his IVs. The KGB agent sat down upon a canvas seat near the front of the cabin. His right hand clutched the pistol with which he had threatened Harland only moments ago.

A glance outside the port window revealed yellow and orange streaks of tracers arcing along the ground below. A trail of burning vehicles marked the rescue force's progress from the south toward the soccer stadium. The park surrounding it was covered with helicopters as men raced toward them like ants towards a picnic. There it was – the last chance of escape – slipping away within sight.

Harland's heart fell as the helicopter pivoted toward the east and its rotors bit into the air. The prospect of survival receded with each mile the helicopter put behind it. Only a grim future of pain and death lay in wait for both Americans.

Boris shouted over the din of the rotors, snagging Harland's attention back to his immediate reality.

"Get to work!"

Harland dug into the bag that Dmitri had prepared for him. His hands wandered over the materials inside – the cold metal of a stethoscope and the soft rolls of gauze. Somewhere underneath the jumble of medical instruments and equipment was his pen for recording vital signs. There seemed little point to writing it all down, given what was about to happen to Colonel Mackinsky. Still, it would keep Harland's mind focused on something besides the prospect of death.

"Ow!"

Cold steel pricked at Harland's index finger. He yanked his hand away and examined the wound. There was just enough light in the cabin to discern the blood dripping freely from the incision. Harland smiled as he realized that Dmitri had left him a parting gift at the bottom of the bag. After giving silent thanks to the old doctor, he dipped his hand in once more and carefully sorted through the contents until he found the scalpel. For a long moment, he held it tight in his hands – as if assuring himself that it was really there.

Harland looked over at Boris as the most basic of plans formed in his mind.

"Help," croaked Harland.

Boris didn't budge.

"I need your help!" Harland shouted. "He's dying!"

The tall KGB agent got to his feet and took a single step toward the back of the compartment.

"What do you mean – dying?!" yelled Boris. "You had better save him or it's your neck! I warned you."

Harland beckoned as he tried his best to appear panicked.

"I need you to do compressions while I breathe for him!"

Boris staggered over toward Mackinsky and pointed at the colonel with his pistol.

"Are you sure?!" he asked.

For the first time, Harland noticed the hint of fear in his voice. The arrogance disappeared along with the mocking sneer. The realization struck Harland like a fist. If Mackinsky dies, Boris is in trouble too. Maybe not as much as me. But enough.

Harland leaned his head down to Mackinsky's chest and listened for a heartbeat. The thumping of the helicopter made it impossible to hear anything without a stethoscope. He shook his head theatrically as if he starred in a medical drama. In rapid-fire English, he spewed out a stream of medical terms that he had learned from watching way too much television. None of it made any sense, and it was hard to keep his face straight as he spoke.

Boris glared at Harland with his bushy eyebrows knitted together in a blend of concern and derision. Harland gestured for him to check the man's heartbeat. When Boris leaned over Mackinsky, Harland took two steps back, pulled the scalpel from his bag, and reached an arm around the Russian's thick neck. The razor-sharp blade bit into Boris' throat. The Russian's right hand flinched as he raised the pistol.

"Drop it!" shouted Harland. To reinforce the point, he dug the scalpel's blade into Boris' skin. A hot trickle of blood flowed down over his fingers. The pistol clattered to the floor.

Harland grabbed a handful of Boris' thick hair and yanked the man's head back. With his other hand on the blade, he shouted in his captive's ear.

"Cockpit!"

Boris complied, taking careful steps toward the front of the cabin. Neither of the flight crew noticed what was happening behind them. Both the pilot and co-pilot seemed more than a little focused on the job of piloting the Hip. When Harland called out to them, the co-pilot jerked his head around. The look of annoyance quickly melted into fear as he realized what was happening.

"Hünfeld!" cried Harland. "Turn back to Hünfeld. I'll kill him!" He brandished the scalpel like a madman and made an exaggerated motion that resembled plunging the blade into Boris' jugular.

The co-pilot smacked the pilot's arm. A backward glance was followed by the rapid tilt of the helicopter. Harland nearly stumbled. Dmitri's arms jerked forward. In a flash, Harland regained his balance and returned the scalpel to the man's throat. Boris became still, but Harland could sense the intent.

The man was like a coiled snake, just looking for the right time to strike. One wrong move and Harland would lose his grip on this tenuous situation.

As the lights of Hünfeld swung into view, Harland gestured at the grounds near the soccer stadium. The Chinooks were already gone but about half a dozen Blackhawks were visible. The fires that dotted the nearby landscape illuminated their bulbous bodies.

"Land near those helicopters!" he shouted.

The Hip picked up speed as it drove straight for the stadium. Harland's breath plunged out in excited waves. He forced himself to remain calm – to not get carried away by the prospect of release from captivity. It was impossible. Soon, this whole miserable experience would be behind him. He couldn't wait.

The helicopter flared to make the landing. Harland stepped back to compensate for the sudden shift. Before his foot landed, Boris spun around. Harland brought the scalpel up just before an elbow smashed into his nose. As Harland staggered backward from the blow, four meaty fingers and a thumb clutched at the sides of his hand. His forearm twisted and a jab of pain brought his entire body to the floor in a smooth downward arc.

Harland sensed the bones in his wrist snapping apart like a fortune cookie. Reluctantly, he opened his hand and let the instrument fall to the floor, where it clanged like a dropped fork at a dinner party. Boris gave out a little triumphant grunt, and Harland took the brief opportunity to throw a punch that glanced off the side of the Russian's head. Boris responded with a fist to the groin. Harland collapsed to his knees and waited for the next blow to land.

Before it hit, something hard struck the helicopter's belly. The airframe trembled. In the very next moment, the transport whirled around on its central axis. Memories of the centrifuge ride at the carnival spilled into his brain. The force threw both men against the walls as the world outside spun around in a blur of dark and light. Harland flailed for a handhold, aware that the ground was coming up fast. One hand caught at the edge of the cargo netting and he held on for dear life.

The force of the impact jarred his spine.

The cockpit disappeared as it smashed into the ground and the whole machine crumpled inwards like an accordion. Harland sensed his body breaking. Bones snapped and tendons tore. The iron taste of blood washed into his mouth. As he lay there bleeding and broken, he heard something stir near the front of the crashed helicopter. It was Boris.

THE GREAT CURVE

The Blackhawks were leaving. White watched the final group of prisoners shepherded toward the waiting helicopters. What was originally supposed to have been a hundred and sixty prisoners had ended up being more than two hundred men. Vital space was taken up by litters for the wounded. The helos weren't cramped. They were overflowing.

In the end, they stopped worrying about troop capacities and just kept piling men on board each machine until the pilot screamed at them to stop. The heavy birds lumbered across the sky and turned west. When all the POWs were gone, White cast a look down from his cupola and hailed Mackinsky.

"Nice work," he said. "What's your status?"

Mackinsky looked away as he spoke. "One KIA before we landed. Twelve KIA prisoners. Thirty-two wounded. Your men did well."

White shrugged. "They're good. Not because of me."

Fitzgerald appeared out of a billowing cloud of smoke. Carrying his rifle and covered in filth, the man looked like a demon emerging from the depths of Hades. Behind him was his platoon of scouts – forty men who had risked everything to come here and pull off a rescue unlike anything attempted before.

"We're all accounted for," said the second lieutenant. Fitzgerald checked his watch then pointed a hand in the direction of the Blackhawks. "Time to move out."

The horizon lit up white to the east, as if someone had just flashed a giant light in their direction. Fitzgerald flinched as the thunder rumbled. His scouts ran for the Blackhawks and boarded. White's crews climbed out of their tanks and did the same.

The skies filled with the drone of a large buzzing insect approaching from the east. White's eyes went wide as he realized the danger and waved the helos off. A Hind could just fire off a volley of rockets to tear through a group of helos sitting on the ground. If Blackhawks took off now, they might stand a chance of surviving.

"Go!" screamed White. "We'll cover you! Go now."

When all of Fox Troop was aboard, the Blackhawks lifted up in unison and scattered. Only White, Fitzgerald, and Mackinsky remained. All three of them understood what needed to be done. They would shoot at the incoming enemy helicopter and draw off its fire from the departing aircraft.

White remounted his tank and fired off his commander's machinegun. The enemy helicopter drew closer, and it became obvious that it wasn't a Hind. That was cold relief. Though its armor was much thinner, the venerable Hip could be armed with rockets and anti-tank weapons. Five hundred meters away, the chopper flared dramatically as if it were a horse throwing off a rider.

Fitzgerald fired the loader's machinegun at the belly of the beast. Tracer rounds danced off the machine and it faltered in mid-air like a runner stumbling on the track. The engine whined as the Hip began a whirling dance of death then plunged downward. Before it crashed, the whole thing teetered toward the front. The rotors dug deep grooves into the ground, then snapped off in huge chunks that were tossed hundreds of yards away from the crash site.

The helicopter did not explode in Hollywood movie fashion, as White had expected. Instead, it sat there inert in the darkness. The three men watched in stifled silence. A sudden downpour quenched the ground. Mackinsky was off - already heading toward the crash site.

White and Fitzgerald jumped down from the tank and ran behind him. The helicopter lay there like a wounded animal. Smoke drifted up from a giant hole in its belly. Mackinsky charged inside with his pistol drawn.

PSYCHO KILLER

"I'm going to kill you."

The words bit through Harland's foggy mind. Something trickled down his face in the darkness and then came a groan from somewhere nearby. One eye opened and he gazed at the faint outlines of the helicopter's wreckage. The interior reeked of aviation fuel and each breath made him dizzy. Harland could feel his pant legs getting soaked, but he was unable to bend his knees. Something heavy lay on top of him, pinning him to the ground.

The gravel voice poured out from the front of the wreck.

"If I must die," said Boris. "I will take you with me."

Lightning flashed outside, briefly painting the interior of the helicopter with a silver flash that cast tall doomsday shadows. Less than a meter away from where Harland lay, the KGB man's face appeared. His eyes were stark-white and he wore a snarling, evil grin. Harland listened to the man slithering forward on his belly. Each glacial movement of the man's huge frame was accompanied by a sick wheeze.

Harland commanded his legs to move, but nothing happened. The lightning flashed again and his eye caught the gleam of something dark and metallic to his right. It was Boris' gun. Right there – just waiting for him.

"This blade," said Boris, "is from a very dear friend of mine. A Vietnamese major.

One of the finest blades I have ever held. Handmade, you understand, by an artisan. He tried to kill me with it, but he was too slow. If he had managed it, I would have been proud to have died from such a blade. Try to think of that as I slide it into your throat."

Harland's hand fumbled along the floor for the pistol. Though he stretched his arms and fingers, it remained inches beyond his grasp. He groaned with effort, but Harland soon understood it was impossible. His legs were broken and his body was entangled in the cargo netting as if he were caught in a giant spiderweb.

Boris cackled. Harland lunged for the gun in vain. Something snapped in his knees. There was no pain – just a chill sensation that beckoned him to sleep and never wake up.

"What's wrong?" asked Boris. "Can't you reach it?" More sick laughter.

"That's…what…your…mother…said last night," croaked Harland.

Boris' face appeared mere inches away. In his hand was a long sleek blade. Harland spit. The slime landed on the big Russian's face. He blinked twice and his mouth curled downward in a pure expression of hatred and disgust.

Boris brought his arm forward in a swift angry motion, plunging the blade directly into Harland's chest. As the life drained from him, Harland heard four quick shots and saw Boris collapse. Boots scrabbled over metal wreckage. Someone shouted.

"Dad? Is that you? Dad. Wake up!"

They were the last words Harland ever heard.

WHAT A DAY THAT WAS

Fitzgerald and White boarded the last flight out of occupied West Germany – it was Crazy Lloyd's Kiowa. They had to stand on the skids and hang on tight to a metal handle near the cockpit. Exhaustion swept over Fitzgerald as the ground whizzed by underneath and the fires of war raged beneath them. He could taste the acrid smoke that clung low to the ground like a fog. The forests that dotted the hills of Fulda burned in the night like row upon row of giant candles.

Though he was tempted more than once to despair at the unprecedented scale of destruction, Fitzgerald understood that the world would somehow survive all this – with or without humanity to witness its rebirth. The thought was oddly comforting and he clung to the notion like a newborn to its mother as they raced through the darkness.

They were shot at several times and more than once, Fitzgerald was convinced he was about to die. The idea of getting killed didn't scare him anymore – nor did he fear the prospect of nuclear devastation. He had done something good in his short life and the future prospect of death in any of its countless forms could never sully that feat. When the bombs fell, the past would remain unsullied by the nuclear fireballs. It was the one thing they couldn't touch.

Before they reached the front lines, the Kiowa veered south and Fitzgerald worried that something had gone wrong.

Was there a mechanical failure? The prospect of getting trapped again was both frightening and welcome at the same time. Something flashed twice in the darkness below and the helicopter slowed its progress and a chill wind whipped at Fitzgerald's body. He clutched the handle as the Kiowa began a quick descent.

When they touched down, Lloyd glanced over at Fitzgerald, who stepped off the skid and planted a foot on solid ground. The Kiowa lifted off again and he felt himself alone in the pitch black as his eyes slowly adjusted to the dark. Gradually, Fitzgerald's eyes adjusted to the dark and he made out the shapes of other men. The wash of the rotors diminished in the distance. He heard voices speaking in low tones while weapons and equipment clinked all around. From behind him, White's twangy voice reached out in a jovial tone.

"Looks like we're all crunchies now, lieutenant," he said. "Gotta say I'm gonna miss having a tank wrapped around me."

A shocked grunt fell from Fitzgerald's mouth.

"Where are we?" Fitzgerald had been too tired to follow the helicopter's route in enough detail to discern their location. Certainly, they were nowhere near Hünfeld, but he couldn't even begin to guess where he stood.

"I'll tell you tomorrow," said White. "All you need to know is we're back in business. We're guerillas now – it's official. Tomorrow we link up with some Territorials and raise hell. Cav style."

Fitzgerald banished a smile with the wipe of his hand and nodded.

"What about weapons? Supplies?" he asked.

"Taken care of," said White. "Evans is at bat for us now. That operation we pulled off back there – it bought him the clout he needed."

So they were now a well-equipped and trained guerilla force. The only thing to really worry about was numbers. Several of his men were in rough shape. The US Army, like any other military force, was fueled by complaints. But the recent grumbling was so bad that Fitzgerald had begun to worry about whether morale had sunk beyond repair. If some of the men had chosen to return to their parent unit back west, he would not have blamed them.

Living as a guerilla fighter was mentally tougher than he had expected. It was not easy to spend one's days in constant fear of discovery and ambush by the Russians.

"How many men agreed?"

White put a hand on his shoulder. "The gang's all here."

Fitzgerald had a million more questions rolling around in his head, but they were all banished with a wide yawn. White threw a sleeping bag at his head and walked off to check on the scouts.

As Fitzgerald lay there on the hard ground, he considered the odds of his surviving the next ten days. He put them at less than ten percent. Peaceful slumber beckoned and he dutifully closed his eyes. Lieutenant Fitzgerald had none of the usual nightmares.

ONCE IN A LIFETIME

The ride to Frankfurtam-Main took all of forty minutes with the helicopter dodging anti-aircraft fire – from both sides – and skirting around the forward edges of the conflict. If Colonel Mackinsky had woken up during the flight and looked down, he would have seen a NATO army in full retreat.

He might have noticed the tanks and men of 1/11 ACR racing back west from Alsfeld, chased all the way to Giessen by the 57th Motorized Rifle Division's lead regiment. A very observant man would have witnessed the ragged elements of the 2/11 ACR and the 8th Infantry Division forming up near the Kinzigsee in an effort to keep the Soviet breakthroughs at bay for just a little longer.

But Colonel Mackinsky saw none of it. He spent the duration of the flight in a dreamless sleep, oblivious to the fighting and dying below. The flight medic, likewise, remained focused on changing the IV bags, checking vital signs, and recording the patient's condition. Things were looking good for the first half of the flight – blood pressure was steadily increasing and the SAT monitor registered a worrisome but not alarming blood-oxygen ratio.

Throughout the ride, Peter sat beside his father and gripped his hand. He was shocked by the frail silent figure who lay on the stretcher without showing any sign of waking. Colonel Ted Mackinsky had loomed like a giant throughout every stage of his son's life.

As a young boy, Peter had listened to his father's stories about fighting the Chinese Communists in the hills and mountains of Korea. Each tale was full of action and characters and absurdity, lending his dad an aura of invincibility and heroism. In elementary school, Peter would repeat the stories to his classmates and teachers. They would politely chuckle and then go back to whatever they had been doing. None of them seemed to understand that his father was a real live hero. The boy became confused and frustrated.

When Peter turned 12 years old, the Vietnam War was in full swing and many Americans questioned their country's participation in the conflict. Upon discovering that his father was serving in Southeast Asia, several of Peter's junior high school classmates asked how his father liked killing babies. One day his father came home on leave for two weeks. When he arrived from the airport, Ted Mackinsky had a stain near the collar of his uniform. Someone had spit on him.

During his teenage years, Peter's relationship with his father grew complicated. The United States had left Vietnam in humiliation and defeat. America had been embroiled in a long and costly conflict that gouged at its social fabric. Everyone just wanted to forget. The US Army was considered a last resort for people with no other options in life. The younger Mackinsky grew skeptical of his father's old war stories. He also wondered about the things that Colonel Mackinsky didn't talk about.

Young and impressionable, Peter bought into the milieu of the day. The new heroes were guys like Bob Woodward, who pursued the truth at any cost and showed the people what was really happening out there. Peter informed his father of his intentions to pursue a career in journalism after high school. He expected his dad to loudly disapprove. Instead, the old man smiled and wished him luck.

"Whatever you do, try to do it well," said his father.

After growing disillusioned with the humdrum grind of being a reporter at the local paper, Peter joined the army. This time, he was sure that his father would beam with pride. Colonel Mackinsky just shook his son's hand and informed him that whatever progress he made in the service would be his own.

No special treatment would be given.

Peter Mackinsky worked harder, ran faster, and shot straighter – all in an attempt to make his old man proud. At the time, the army was undergoing a fundamental change in the way it trained its men.

The draft was long gone. No longer would rampant drug use and criminal gangs be tolerated. It was 1981 and the newly elected president wasted no time in crafting a budget aimed at reforming the American military into the world's best fighting force. Mackinsky saw something of his father in the country's newest leader and redoubled his efforts to meet the higher standards.

After earning a place among the elite, Peter wore his uniform home and told his father of the new posting. His unit was filled with the best and brightest that the army had to offer. Their assignments would be dangerous and the stakes would be higher than ever. Just as before, Ted Mackinsky returned the news with a polite smile. Peter exploded. He stood there in the living room and loudly demanded to know what it would take to make the old man proud.

Ted Mackinsky set the newspaper down, got up off the recliner and bear hugged Peter.

"Son, I was proud of you from the day you were born," he said. "Go make yourself proud."

The last ten minutes of the helicopter ride were spent in decline. The vitals took a steady journey downward and the flight medic was forced to compensate. The IV drip was opened up while a rebreather oxygen mask replaced the nasal cannula. Though the shaking of the helicopter rotors made it nearly impossible to find the man's blood pressure, three tries were enough to find that the systolic was dropping like a lead balloon.

Colonel Mackinsky's barrel chest rose and fell in sporadic rapid motions. It was clear that the man was dying. Peter squeezed the old man's hand and begged his father to fight.

"Hang in there, dad!" he said. "We're nearly there."

As the helicopter landed, the flight medic handed his report to the doctor and gave the nurse a quick briefing while Ted Mackinsky was thrown on a stretcher and wheeled into the operating room. Peter Mackinsky watched his father disappear inside and prayed harder than he had ever prayed in his entire life.

Hours later, the doors swung open and the surgical team staggered out. The head surgeon approached Peter and removed his mask. His face was etched with deep lines of fatigue.

"Your father fought like a lion in there," he said. "But in the end, we couldn't save him. There was just too much trauma. I'm sorry."

Peter thanked the doctor and asked if he could say goodbye. The surgeon gestured toward the operating room.

The OR was freezing. His father lay in the center of the room, resting on the table. A sheet was pulled up over his head. Peter slid it back gently as he looked down on the gaunt expressionless face of his greatest hero. Finally alone, he found the strength to let his emotions go. After a few minutes, the flood passed and he drew a palm down his wet face.

"Dad, I'm so sorry," he said. "I tried so hard but I couldn't save you. I tried so hard."

The moment of regret soon passed, replaced by fond memories of time spent together in the woods near their home. There was fishing and hunting. There were games of touch football on Thanksgiving. And though the man he had shared these with had now passed, they still lingered on in the son's heart.

Peter let go of his father's hand and walked out of the sterile room, carrying all of these gifts inside.

EPILOGUE: DON'T WORRY ABOUT THE GOVERNMENT

Olney Federal Support Center
Laytonsville, Maryland

When the knock came, CIA Director David Heath got up from the desk and straightened his tie before answering the door. Tracton stood there with a few days of stubble peeking out from his chin. Instead of a suit, he was wearing jeans and polo shirt. The tight regulations on water use in the emergency bunker had made it nearly impossible to shave or wash clothes on a regular basis. Everything had become very casual down here since the war started. Heath briefly wondered if it was the same for all Washington bureaucrats since being whisked away to underground sites just like this one.

"Keith! Come on in! How's it going?" Heath flashed a smile and waved the man inside.

Tracton stepped forward but refused the offered seat. Instead, he folded his arms and shot a glance at the clock.

"What's this all about, Dave? I'm pretty busy these days."

Since the war had begun, the two men had strenuously avoided each other. Tracton had blamed Heath for an alarmist presidential briefing that had essentially started World War III. Heath had balked at the suggestion. If anything, they hadn't pushed hard enough in the early years of the administration.

If the Soviets had understood from the very start that America meant business, they would never have considered attacking the West.

Heath gulped down his pride. "Look, Keith. I know we've had our differences. I'm sorry about that. I think we should let bygones be bygones. What do you say?"

Tracton pursed his lips in disapproval. "I don't know what to say, to be honest. I told you not to push too hard, but you just wouldn't listen. And now look at where we are." He gestured to the blank windowless walls and the rusting army cot in the corner of the office.

Heath held his palms out as if in surrender. "Okay. Okay. You have a point. But you've seen the evidence too. The Russians were planning something long before that briefing. The war was coming our way regardless. I'll concede I could have communicated things better."

Tracton sighed and sat on the cot. "So what is it you need me for? We're knee-deep in signals analysis right now. There's not a thing I can do to help you guys."

Heath fumbled with a package of stale crackers that were dated back to the 1960s and offered one to Tracton. He refused.

"The war is going bad for us, Keith," he said. "I've seen the Pentagon briefings. Sat in on a few. We're looking real hard at losing Europe. No one's said it yet, but it's there."

Tracton snorted. "The old man will drop a big one before that happens. You'll see. The Russians will cave. All my sources-."

"Have you looked at White Lily lately?" said Heath. He reached into his desk and pulled out a folder. On the top of it was stamped "TOP SECRET" in red ink. Inside the folder were transcriptions of a secret wire tap that the United States had placed on Soviet underwater communication cables in the Barents Sea. It was a joint military-CIA-NSA mission that had run for over ten years now. It had gleaned more intelligence about the Russians than any single intelligence operation in history.

"I've been busy," replied Tracton.

"Well that's too bad," said Heath. "Because the Russians are talking about moving their ballistic missile submarines out of their bastions."

Tracton stood up. "They're getting ready to strike?!"

Heath bit into a stale cracker and cracked open a Tab. He took a gulp and swirled it around his mouth as if he were tasting wine at a fancy restaurant.

"Ahhhh…1965. An excellent vintage…No, Keith. They're not going to hit us first. At least not yet. But they will if we start in with the nukes. From what I've heard from my analysts, it seems they're ready to go the whole distance at the first hint of a strike. They're playing to win, my friend. These guys will never accept second place."

"What do you suggest?" asked Tracton. "How do we get out of this without ending the whole world. I'd kinda like to see the sun again, Dave. I think everyone in here would like that."

Heath banged his palms on the edge of his desk and smiled. "We give it to them."

"WHAT?!"

Heath chuckled. "Hear me out! We give them a military victory that we would never wish on our worst enemy. They occupy Western Europe for the next ten years. Let them fight a losing war just like the one in Afghanistan. Only this time, it's not villagers armed with Kalashnikovs – it's well-trained men with the latest military gear. The United States, in the meantime, waits it out and watches the Soviet regime implode just as we predicted. When the time is right, we step in and take back what's ours."

Tracton swiped a palm over his face. "You're crazy. Even if that was a good idea, the president would never go for it. We have allies and interests to protect. We just need to keep inflicting losses until the Soviets understand that they can never win. A ceasefire can work. We're already talking. Backchannels-."

"Forget it," said Heath. He patted the White Lily folder. "The real answers are in here. You're listening to wishful thinking again."

Tracton sighed. "Tell me – how did you come up with this idea? Why do you think it's going to work? Guerilla actions in occupied Europe. Come on. You're talking about Operation Gladio."

"Not Gladio!" shouted Heath. "I've closed it down. We tried it and it was a dead end. The president was pretty disappointed at the results. I'm in the doghouse right now.

What I'm talking about is setting up stay-behind military units to strike at the Warsaw Pact. Drain them at every opportunity. We can land our guys in there. Supply them just like we did with the Contras. Europe is huge. Trust me on this."

"You really think it's going to work?"

"I know it will," said Heath. He brought out another report and slapped it on his desk. "Operation Firefox. Look at these guys. A single cavalry troop behind enemy lines wiped out a ton of Russians. With the help of a few planes, they did more damage to the Soviet offensive in thirty minutes than a division's worth of regular infantry. And then! And then they raided a POW camp. Rescued two hundred guys! Look at this. It's the future!"

Tracton snatched the folder from Heath's desk. His eyes widened as he skimmed the after-action reports and gazed at the photos of a destroyed airfield.

"You have these guys operating under CIA authority?" asked Tracton.

"Not ours. DIA," muttered Heath. "They don't wanna share. Too greedy."

"And so what do you need me for – oh no. Dammit, Dave! I should have known."

Heath shrugged. "We're sidelined here," he said. "Since the war began, I'm running shoestring ops in East Germany with guys who haven't shot a gun in twenty years. Bottom of the barrel. I need a way back in. This is it. I just need your help on this one. I'll never ask you for another favor again. Please!"

Tracton rolled his eyes and thumbed through the photographs again. Heath paused for long enough to let the idea sink in.

"What's your timeline on this?" asked Tracton.

"Today," said Heath. "Immediately. All I need is-"

Tracton put up a hand. "Yes, yes – you need me to create a new layer of bureaucracy in the NSA and declare a liaison with your agency and the DIA. Assign it a joint mission without informing the military and staff it with some non-existent personnel. Boom – the president authorizes CIA access to requisite Defense Intelligence assets. Am I right?"

"I wouldn't put it exactly that way," said Heath. "But you got the gist of it. So…whaddya say?"

"You really want to get into the business of creating a guerilla army?" asked Tracton.

Heath nodded. "I do. Even if we win this war and I'm wrong, what harm does it do?"

Tracton grabbed a cracker and chomped down on it.

"You owe me for this," he said. "Big time."

US PLAN OF ATTACK – OPERATION FIRST STRIKE

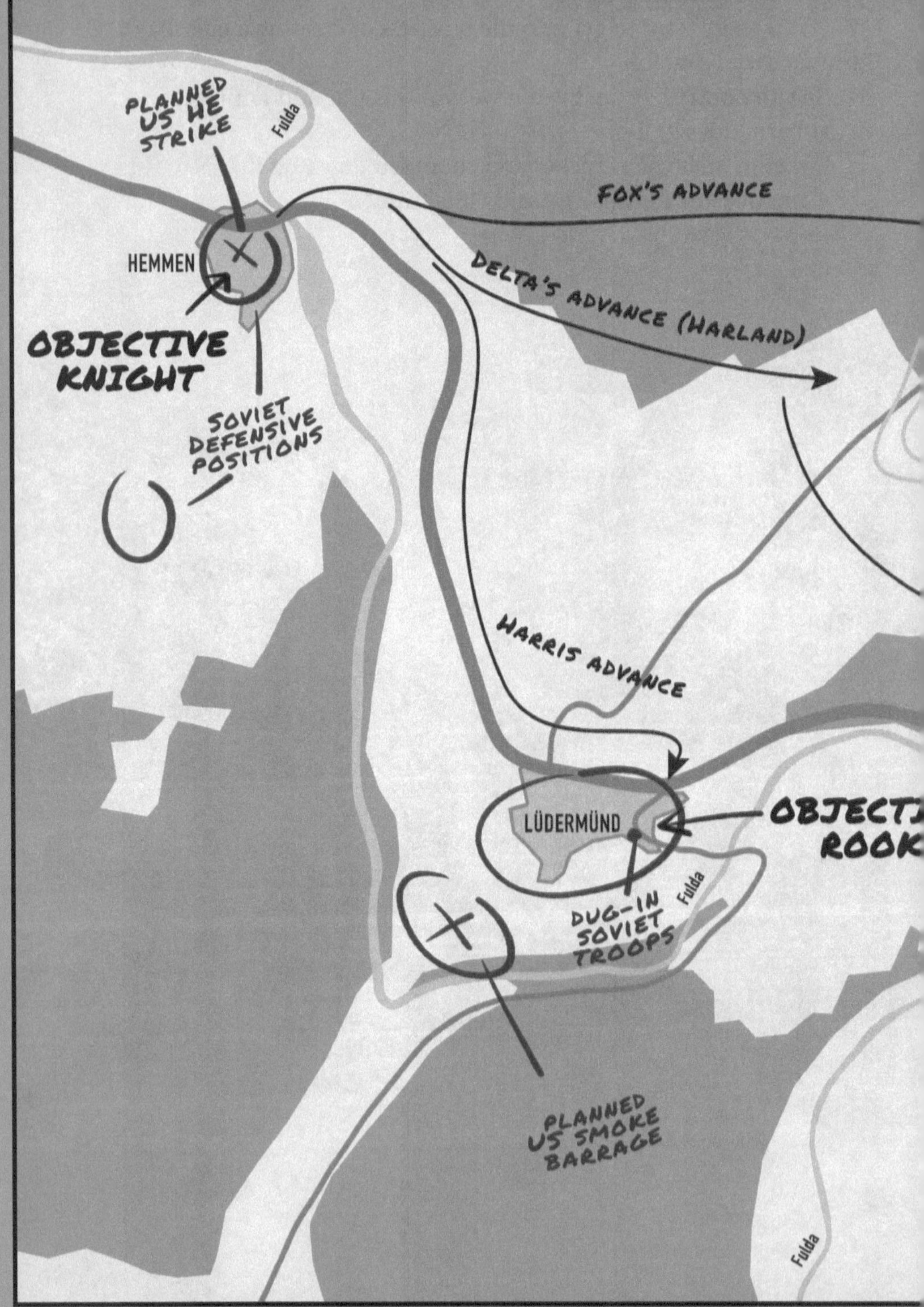

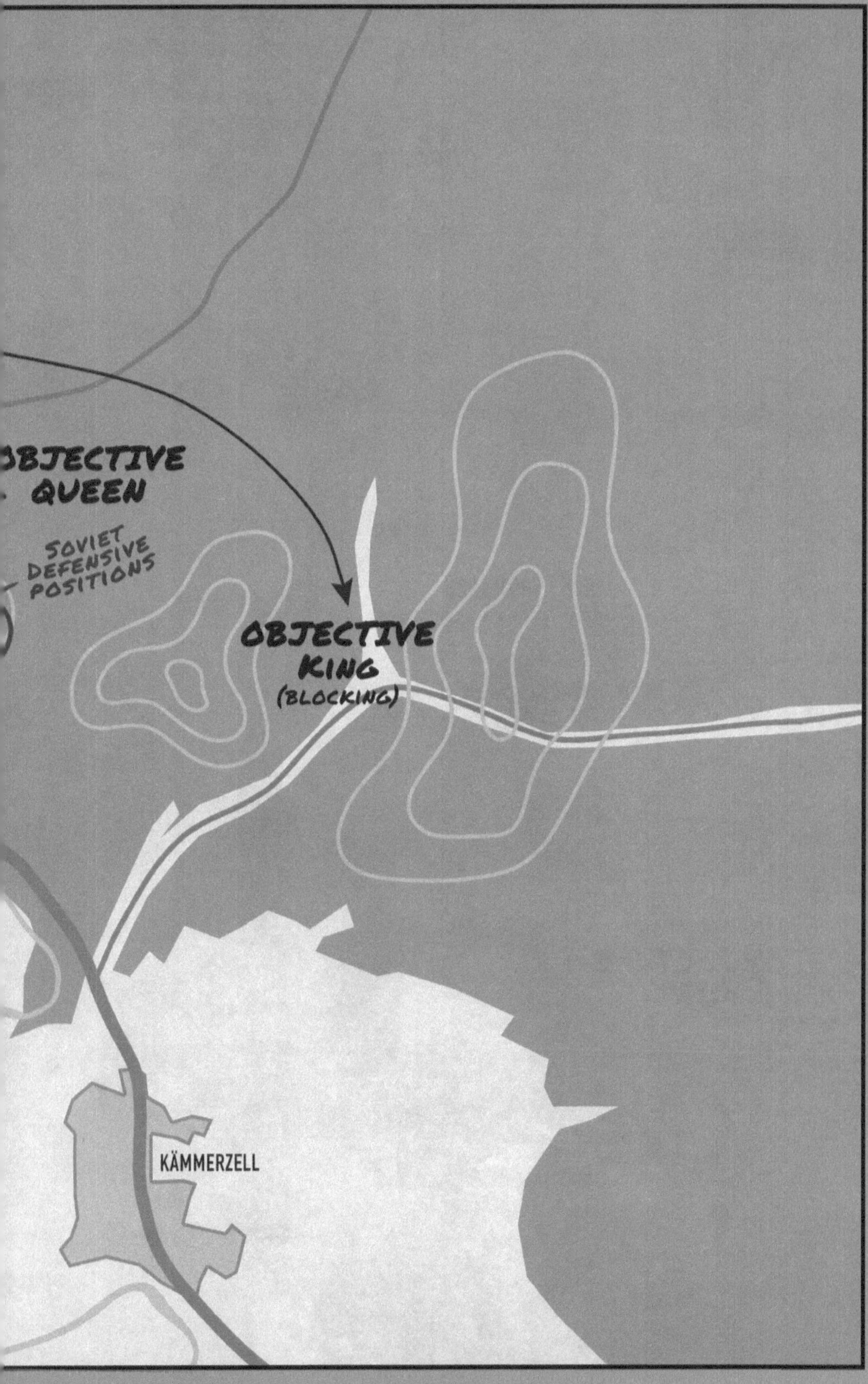

OBJECTIVE
QUEEN
SOVIET
DEFENSIVE
POSITIONS
OBJECTIVE
KING
(BLOCKING)
KÄMMERZELL

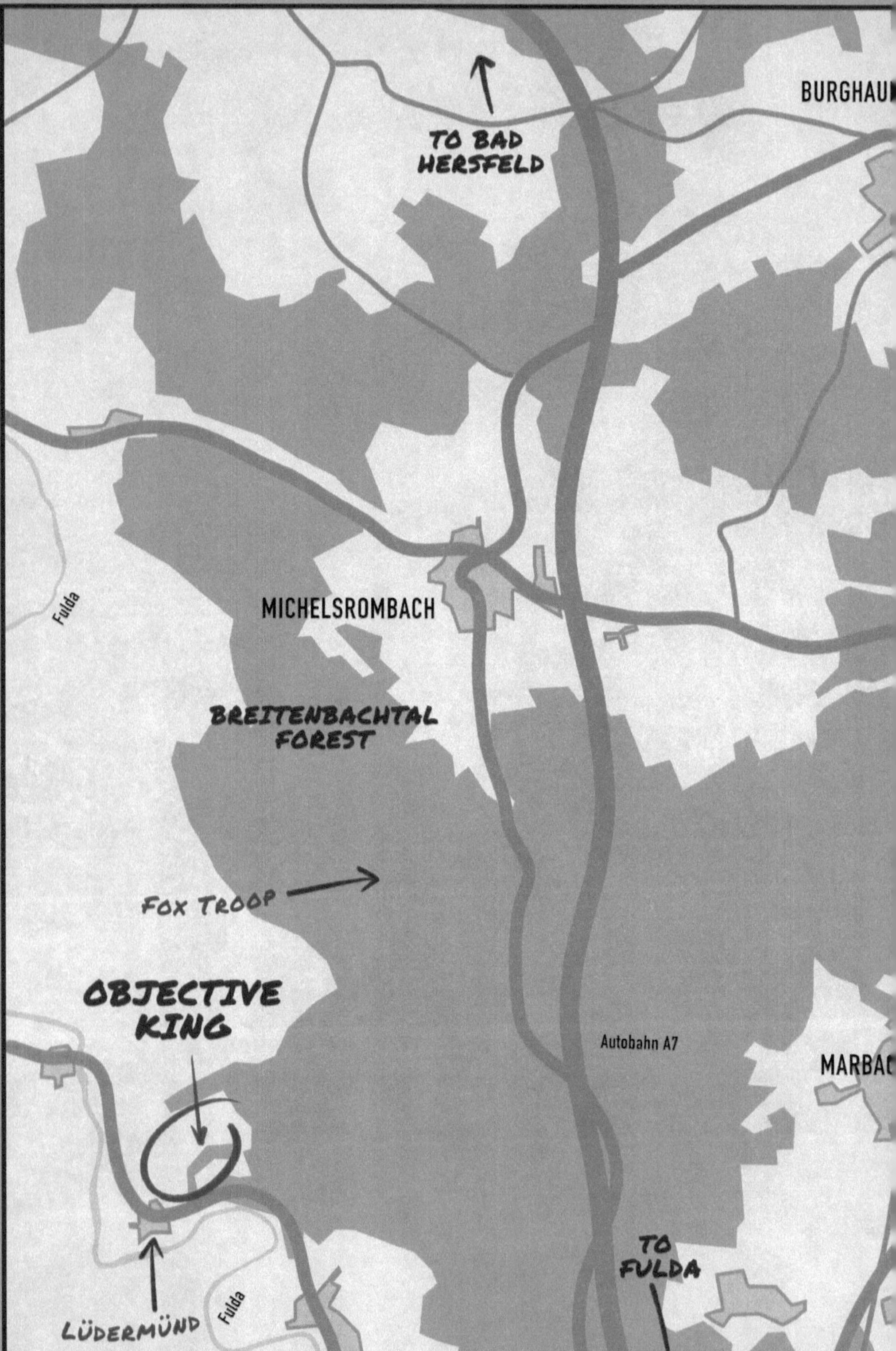

TO BAD HERSFELD
BURGHAU
MICHELSROMBACH
Fulda
BREITENBACHTAL FOREST
FOX TROOP
OBJECTIVE KING
Autobahn A7
MARBAC
TO FULDA
LÜDERMÜND
Fulda

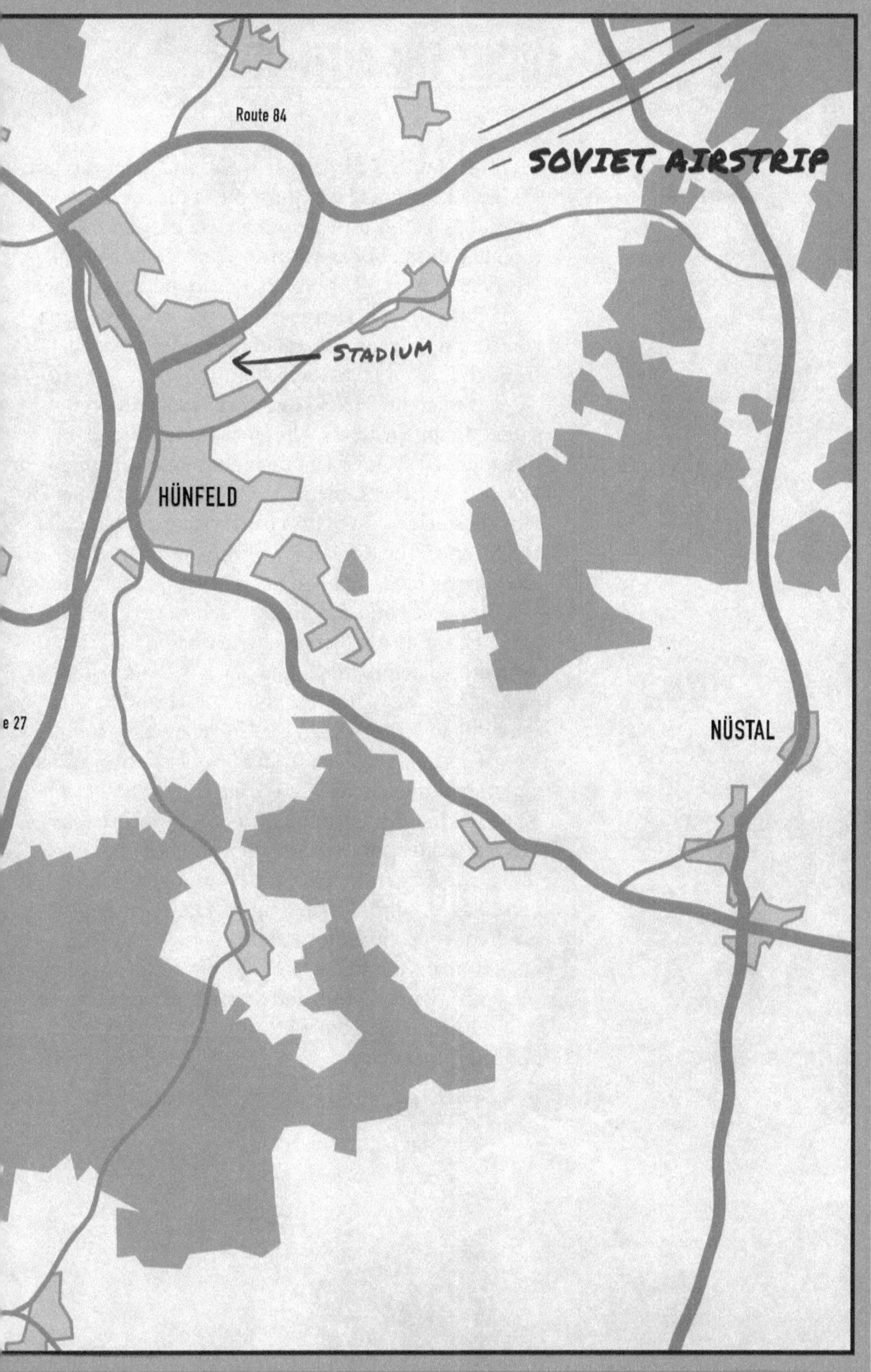

Route 84
SOVIET AIRSTRIP
STADIUM
HÜNFELD
e 27
NÜSTAL

ABOUT THE AUTHOR

Brad Smith is a freelance writer and game designer. He has a keen interest in the topic of the late Cold War, which has fed his creative output. He has authored around a dozen books set in an alternate World War III: 1985 universe. His blog can be found at: www.hex-sides.com. You can also access his books on the Amazon.com store page. Several of his stories are available through Lock 'n Load Publishing.

His main interests are writing, wargaming, and spending time with his wife and son. He recently designed "NATO Air Commander" and the soon to be released "That Others May Live" both published by Hollandspiele. Two of his favorite wargames are "Gulf Strike" and "The Korean War" from Victory Games. His gaming blog can be found at: www.hexsides.com.

Brad has worked as an Emergency Medical Responder in Canada then as a writer based in Geneva, Switzerland before moving to Japan in 2004, where he has lived ever since. He holds a Bachelor's degree majoring in History from the University of Winnipeg, a Master's in Journalism from the University of British Columbia, and a dual Master's degree in TESOL and Applied Linguistics from the University of Leicester. He has written for academic journals, newspapers, radio, and magazines on a variety of topics. He recently served as an editor for an issue of Yaah! magazine and is a frequent contributor to other game journals.

His main writing inspirations include Tom Clancy, Joe Scalzi, Ralph Peters, and Stephen King. His favorite books include "Red Storm Rising", "Old Man's War", and "Red Army".

ABOUT THE EDITOR
- Hans Korting -

I have been reading books about (military) aviation history all of my life, and this way the connection with military history is easily made. Main interest is WWII, but I also enjoy reading up on and playing games about WWI, modern-era warfare, the American Civil War, Napoleonics, and more. First game ever was bought in an American book store in Amsterdam, Avalon Hill's D-Day '77. Next game was SPI's Arnhem, and a whole range of games has followed since. Putting my hands, or rather eyes, where my mouth is, I next decided to help out proofreading rulebooks. Some gaming magazines were next, like War Diary magazine. I also write about boardwargames for Ducosim's (DutchConflictSimulation) Spel! magazine, and sometimes try to write a decent article for a magazine too. Daytime job is at a small insurance broker as a claims handler.

AUDIO BOOK EDITION
- Narrated By: Othello Lofton -

Othello Lofton was an audiobook narrator before audiobooks were a thing. As a child he spent many a weekend afternoon in the library or cruising the flea market for used paperbacks of the SF persuasion. He would then spend the rest of the week, reading his treasures out loud, voicing the characters and reenacting their adventures. Nowadays, you'll find this self-professed comic book nerd in his home studio, The Danger Room, reliving those childhood stories in front of a microphone. And he's glad you decided to come along on the adventure.

WHAT IS THE WORLD AT WAR 85 GAME SERIES
- by David Heath -

I am the Director of Operations at Lock 'n Load Publishing, where we produce both tabletop and computer games with a strategy theme. So what made us publish a book of short stories? The love of gaming. These short stories were inspired by the kind of stories friends share about games they played and the adventures they experienced while playing them. Those stories always remind me of the kind told by my Dad, his friends, and my own buddies who spent time in the service.

The idea for this book series started from a long desire to hear the stories of other gamers, and to share my love for gaming. This project became real thanks to Brad Smith, Hans Korting, Keith Tracton, and many others. Without their support this never would have happened. While talking this over it became clear we weren't the only ones who enjoyed telling and listening to gaming adventures.

This story use a number of things from our World at War 85 game series, specifically the names units and even the occasional moments inspired by game events. This added a new level to our stories and added the ability and similarity for these men to live on in each of our games.

Some of you may be wondering what the World at War 85 game series is all about. The World at War 85 (WaW85) series is a dynamic platoon-level tactical combat board game series centered on armored combat from the 1980s in a fictional World War III setting. With unparalleled artwork and a formation based game mechanic that keeps both players constantly involved, each action-packed engagement plays out cinematically. Decisions need to be made quickly. Tactical leadership is key. Unique abilities and synergies enhance effectiveness. And detailed objectives based ont he scenario layout encourages bold gameplay. There is even a Solo module for those quiet nights at home.

Platoon combat is central to WaW85, but besides Heavy Armor and Soft Armor units, we have Support Weapon such as mortars, heavy machine guns, and anti-tank guns. There are also Helicopters, faction Leaders, fixed-wing Close Air Support and an in depth suit of Artillery options, both on and off-board. Individuals such as Leaders, Special Weapons Teams, and, of course, Special Forces, complete the forces available for each side. We also have free downloadable game walkthroughs, making the game series more accessible to new players more than ever.

Whether you are a fan of 80s-era military fiction or the World War 3 setting, the WaW85 series has you covered with a variety of boxed games and expansions, including an evolving storyline to follow as you play through ear game in the series. With WaW85 the gaming never ends. It's Platoon-level tactical combat at its best!

HEROES AGAINST THE RED STAR

The Red Star Strikes!

It's the spring of 1985 and the Cold War has turned Hot. Out of the dawn sky, Soviet paratroopers are being whisked across the West German border. On the ground, the 1st Tank Division and 33rd Motor Rifle Regiment are rolling toward key command-and-control targets. NATO has to mobilize quickly. World War III has begun, and once again Western Europe is the focal point.

In Heroes Against the Red Star, the Lock 'n Load Tactical Series presents the sweeping rush of the Soviet Red Army, from the shock of the ambitious opening offensive on May 14th against American-held positions in West Germany to the furious rush to Paris, in June, against emboldened French forces

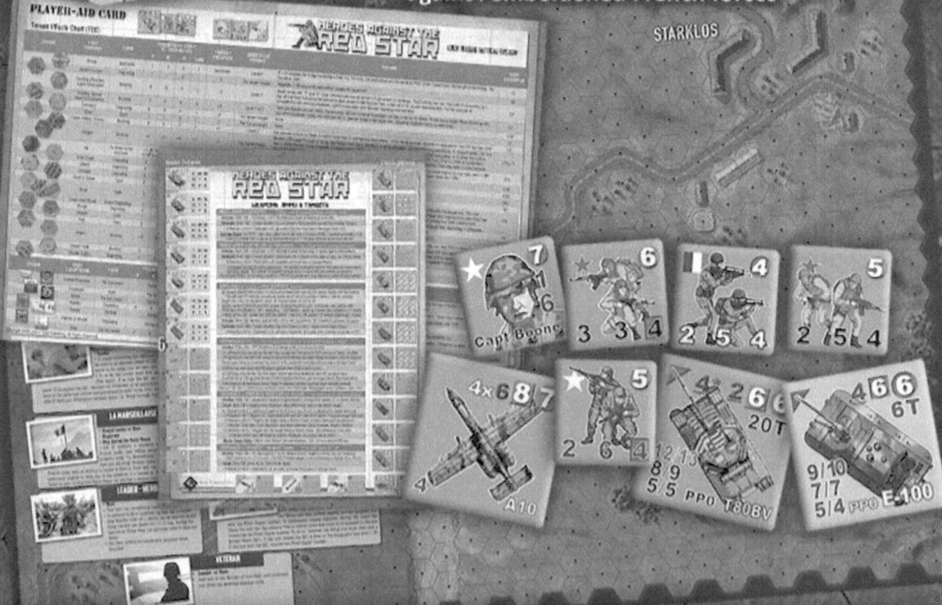